EGYPTIAN CHRONICLES

THE HORNED VIPER

Hopi and Isis can remember the terrible accident on the River Nile when they lost their parents to crocodiles. Hopi still bears crocodile teethmarks on his leg. But five years have passed, and they've been lucky: eleven-year-old Isis is a beautiful dancer, and she's been spotted by a dance and music troupe in the town of Waset. Now they live with the troupe, and Isis performs regularly. Meanwhile, thirteen-year-old Hopi, marked by the gods, pursues his strange connection with dangerous creatures . . .

Join them in the world of ancient Egypt as they uncover the dark deeds happening around them. If there's anything you don't understand, you may find an explanation at the back of the book.

Also by Gill Harvey

Egyptian Chronicles series
The Spitting Cobra

Coming soon
The Sacred Scarab
The Deathstalker

Also available
Orphan of the Sun

EGYPTIAN CHRONICLES

THE HORNED VIPER

GILL HARVEY

BLOOMSBURY

LONDON BERLIN NEW YORK

Bloomsbury Publishing, London, Berlin and New York

First published in Great Britain in 2009 by Bloomsbury Publishing Plc
36 Soho Square, London, W1D 3QY

A CIP catalogue record of this book is available from the British Library

ISBN 978 0 7475 9564 9

FSC
Mixed Sources
Product group from well-managed
forests and other controlled sources
Cert no. SGS - COC - 2061
www.fsc.org
© 1996 Forest Stewardship Council

Typeset by Dorchester Typesetting Group Ltd
Printed in Great Britain by Clays Ltd, St Ives plc

1 3 5 7 9 10 8 6 4 2

www.bloomsbury.com/childrens
www.bloomsbury.com/gillharvey

For Mala

CONTENTS

PROLOGUE

Sweat ran down the men's backs. It trickled down their foreheads and into their eyes. The ropes chafed their shoulders and hands, cutting into their flesh, so that blood mingled with the sweat.

'*Heave!*' shouted Hat-Neb, the overseer.

The men heaved, and the huge block of stone inched up the ramp.

'Useless! It's hardly moved! *Heave!*' yelled Hat-Neb. He turned to his deputy. 'What's that you've got in your hand?'

'A whip, sir.' The deputy looked troubled.

'Then why aren't you using it?' Hat-Neb's face was twisted with fury. 'These men are useless, lazy good-for-nothings. Whip them!'

The deputy looked uneasy. 'Sir, they're doing their best. Five men fell sick yesterday and cannot work.

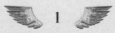 1

Those that are here haven't rested since dawn.'

Hat-Neb narrowed his eyes. 'Are you disobeying me?'

The deputy said nothing. He wiped a hand across his forehead, then, reluctantly, he raised his whip and turned towards the men. The whip whistled through the air, and the men cried out in pain. The block of stone shifted a tiny bit further up the ramp.

The temple was half built. It would be beautiful when it was finished, glistening with white paint overlaid with brilliant colours. Its images and hieroglyphs would all speak of the glory of Horus, the king of the gods.

But the building process wasn't such a beautiful sight. Things were falling behind, because a nasty sickness was spreading among the men. It made them vomit and sweat, and it left them weak and shaking. They needed to rest for several days before they could work again. But Hat-Neb was cruel and merciless. He had no sympathy. He just worked the other men harder and harder until some of them thought they would die of exhaustion.

The deputy raised his whip again, but he didn't crack it. He could see that the men were close to breaking. In fact, they were so exhausted that there was a risk they would let go of the rope altogether.

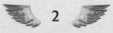

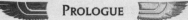

'Steady, men!' he shouted. 'Hold it there!' He turned to Hat-Neb and spoke urgently, 'Sir, we need to give them a rest. The stone is unstable – we must secure it –'

He spoke too late. The men had lost control of the rope. Their muscles were too tired to hold on any longer and the massive stone was beginning to slip. They cried out in agony as the rope ripped through their hands, tearing their skin. And the stone moved faster, faster, faster down the slope.

The next few seconds passed in a blur. The stone continued to plummet. The men at the top of the ramp looked down in horror. Meanwhile Ipuy, a young scribe, hurried towards the overseer to deliver a report, his head bent with busy thoughts. He didn't see the stone. The deputy opened his mouth to shout.

'Ipuy!'

Ipuy glanced up at the ramp. It was the last thing he would ever see – the ramp, and the massive block of limestone that was about to snuff out his life. He gave a short, final scream. And then he was dead.

For one instant, silence fell as dust settled and the men stood still in shock. It was the deputy who moved first, hurtling towards the great stone and the young man who lay beneath it. His heart was already bursting with grief.

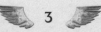

'No! No, no!' he cried. 'Not Ipuy. Please, please not Ipuy . . .'

But all that could be seen of Ipuy was one leg, jutting out from beneath the stone. There was no hope, no hope at all. The deputy sank to the ground, and clutched that one foot and leg, soaking it in tears. Ipuy had been his best friend.

It was some time before the men could tear him away. But the stone had to be lifted, and the body pulled out. The deputy looked up to see Hat-Neb shouting orders.

'Stop gawping!' he barked. 'Anyone would think you'd never seen a corpse before! Form two lines and start lifting!'

The deputy gazed at him through his watery eyes. *I hate you*, he thought. *You have brought nothing but hardship and misery to me and my men. Now you have killed my best friend. I hate you. And if it's the last thing I do, I will get my revenge.*

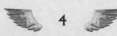

CHAPTER ONE

'I'm afraid that will be quite impossible,' said Paneb. 'We have two young children. It would be very difficult to take them on such a trip.'

'Ah, now that's a shame. A real shame.' The visitor stroked his chin. 'I'd heard that you are the best dance and music troupe in Waset. I only employ the best. And I pay the best prices.'

Isis sat quietly in the corner, holding her breath. What would Paneb say now? The visitor wanted to take the troupe upriver on his new boat, but she really hoped Paneb would say no. She *really* didn't want to go. The River Nile filled her with terror.

Paneb exchanged glances with his wife Nefert, then smiled politely. 'I'm glad you've heard good things about us,' he said. 'If we could stay here in Waset, we would say yes at once. But a long trip like

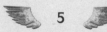

that . . .' He shook his head. 'It can't be done. I'm sorry.'

A flicker of annoyance passed over the visitor's face. He was a big, fat man. Isis guessed that he was very rich. His clothes and wig were of the finest quality, and the room was full of his heavy perfume. A tall, strong fan-bearer stood just behind him, gently waving an ostrich-feather fan. The man seemed to be thinking.

'I don't need the whole troupe,' he said. 'You have a number of musicians.' He nodded at Sheri and Kia, Nefert's widowed sisters. 'And you have two dancers.' He smiled at Isis and her dance partner, Mut.

Isis lowered her gaze in despair. *No. Not us. Anyone but us*, she thought.

'Two musicians, two dancers,' continued the man. 'That would be perfect! Your dancers are beautiful. I will pay double your usual price. And, of course, their passage back to Waset from Djeba.'

Silence fell. Isis could see what Paneb and Nefert were thinking. It was too good to refuse.

'Well . . .' began Paneb. Isis caught his eye, pleading with him to say no. He looked troubled. 'That is a very attractive offer. But there is another problem.'

The man raised an eyebrow. 'Yes? Tell me. I'm sure there's nothing I can't resolve.'

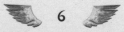

'One of our dancers is afraid of the river. Her parents were taken to the Next World by crocodiles, you see.'

The man looked from Isis to Mut and back again. Isis swallowed in fear as the man sized her up.

'Does he mean you, little one?' he asked, his voice surprisingly gentle.

Isis nodded. The man stepped towards her. He placed a hand on her head and gazed deep into her eyes.

'What is your name?' he asked.

'Isis.' It came out in a whisper.

'Isis . . . the greatest goddess of them all,' he murmured. 'Well, Isis, I hate to hear of anyone living in fear. We must seek the blessing of the gods so that you are freed of it.' He smiled, and cupped her face in his hands. 'Believe me. You will be safe on my boat.'

Isis looked up at him, entranced by the power he seemed to exude. To her surprise, she felt her fear melting away.

'The only question is this: whose blessing must we seek?' continued the man.

Isis thought about it. There was Hapi, the god of the Nile itself, who brought the blessing of the annual flood. But Sobek, the crocodile god, was the one she feared most.

'Sobek,' she managed to say.

'Very well. Then we shall offer a couple of nice fat lambs to Sobek. And may his protection be upon us all.'

Isis stared in disbelief. Two whole lambs! This man really *was* rich . . . he could do anything he wanted! She felt almost dizzy. Then, suddenly, she came to her senses. She never went anywhere without her brother Hopi.

'But I can't go unless Hopi comes, too,' she blurted out.

The man looked at her in surprise. 'And who is Hopi?'

'He's my brother,' Isis said, and pointed to where the slight form of Hopi stood near the doorway, a deep frown on his face.

Hopi limped along the streets of Waset, feeling fed up. A trip to Djeba was the last thing he wanted to do, especially with that man Hat-Neb and his fan-bearer. He didn't like the look of either of them. But he didn't want Isis to go on her own, either. His sister had been terrified of the river ever since that day five years ago, when crocodiles had killed their parents. They had almost killed Hopi, too.

He turned down a little side street and knocked on

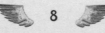

a door. After a moment, a wizened old man peered out of the whitewashed house.

'Good afternoon, Menna. May the gods be with you,' Hopi greeted him.

'Hopi. May the gods be with you, too. Come in.' Menna opened the door wider and Hopi stepped inside. The old priest led the way through to a court-yard at the back.

'Sit down, sit down,' said Menna, waving his hand at some mats in the shade. 'Now, what have you brought today?'

Hopi usually arrived with a snake or scorpion that he had caught, but today he shook his head. 'Nothing but bad news.'

'Bad news! Why, what has happened? Is someone sick?'

'Oh, not that bad.' Hopi felt slightly ashamed. 'I have to go on a trip, Menna. A rich overseer has a new boat, and he's hired some of the troupe to entertain him while he travels back to the temple he's working on at Djeba. So I have to accompany Isis.'

'And what's so terrible about that?'

'I am learning so much from you. I would rather stay here.'

Menna smiled. 'I am not the only source of know-ledge, Hopi,' he said. 'It is good to travel. Don't rely

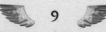

only on an old man like me.'

Hopi tried to feel less dejected, but it was difficult. Becoming Menna's apprentice had changed his life. It had given him a future. There weren't many jobs that a cripple could do, especially a cripple with little learning. But now he knew that one day he would become a priest of Serqet, with the authority to treat the bites and stings of dangerous snakes and scorpions.

'I suppose you're right,' he said reluctantly.

'Of course I am,' said Menna. 'When do you leave?'

'Tomorrow, I think.'

'Then what are you doing here?' exclaimed the old man. 'Go, Hopi! Make your preparations. Enjoy yourself. When you return, you can come and tell me what you have learned. You might even be able to teach me something.'

'Impossible,' said Hopi, smiling a little. 'Very well, Menna. I will do as you say.'

The old man ushered him out on to the street. Hopi said his farewells and began to walk home. Then he changed his mind. If he was going to embark on this journey, he wanted to take a look at the boat that would carry him.

The riverbank at Waset was busy. Fishing boats dotted the shore; the wooden ferry that carried

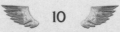

people over to the west bank was just coming in. In one section of the harbour, there was a little line of pleasure boats owned by the rich men of the town. Among them was one that Hopi had never seen before. It was shaped in a curve, with the prow and stern both high out of the water. Two big rudder-paddles dug into the water at the stern, and strong square sails were furled on its masts. In the middle there was an ornate cabin to provide shelter from the sun, and at the prow there was another open-sided shelter for passengers to sit in.

Hopi stared at it. This boat was bigger and more beautiful than any of the others. For the first time, he began to feel that the trip wouldn't be too bad after all. There were men on board, and he watched as one of them climbed down a little ladder to the shore.

'Is this the boat of Hat-Neb?' Hopi asked, as the man passed by.

'Why, what do you know about it?' asked the man sourly.

'If it is, I'm coming on board tomorrow,' said Hopi.

The man narrowed his eyes. 'Are you indeed? And who are you?'

Hopi explained about the dance troupe. 'I'm Hopi, the brother of one of the dancers, and a trainee priest of Serqet,' he finished.

'A priest of Serqet? You deal with snakes and scorpions?'

'That's right,' said Hopi. 'I'm the apprentice of Menna, the greatest priest in the whole of Waset.'

'Is that so?' said the man, and Hopi saw that he was impressed. 'In that case, I'm sure there are many things we can teach each other. I am Tutmose, one of the doctors of the royal court.'

Hopi's heart gave a leap. A royal doctor! Menna had been right. Perhaps he would learn many things on this trip. He smiled. 'That is good news, sir.'

'Indeed.' Tutmose nodded briskly. 'I shall look forward to spending many hours with you.'

'Thank you, sir.' Hopi felt overwhelmed.

Tutmose patted him on the shoulder, then hurried on into the streets of Waset. Hopi watched him go, feeling ten times lighter. Things were definitely looking up.

The chief priest raised his knife, and Isis saw the flash of the blade in the sunlight. He brought it down and with one clean, smooth movement, he slit the lamb's throat. There was a brief gurgling, rasping sound as the creature sank to the ground and kicked its legs in its dying throes. Then it was still. Isis felt sick. But as the priest carried out the ritual on the second lamb,

she calmed down. It was all so quick, and there was surprisingly little blood.

'All over.' Hat-Neb smiled at Isis.

Isis smiled back at him, full of gratitude. Hat-Neb was a man of his word, and had wasted no time in buying the two lambs he had promised to sacrifice. There was no major temple to the god Sobek in Waset, but there was a little shrine on the outskirts of the town, close to the river. With Mut and Hopi, Sheri and Kia, Isis had accompanied Hat-Neb and his fan-bearer to the site of the shrine, where they were watching at a distance. Two whole lambs for her sake! She felt like a princess.

Three other priests set to work on the lamb carcasses, expertly carving them up.

'Come. We can go to the pool now,' said Hat-Neb.

He began to walk slowly around the shrine with his fan-bearer one pace behind him. The group followed as Hat-Neb led them along a little path shaded with date palms. Ahead, Isis caught a glimpse of shimmering water, and her heart thudded with fear.

The sacred pool was muddy, its banks a tangle of reeds. The surface of the water was calm, with just a tiny ripple drifting across it when the breeze blew. Isis looked around anxiously for Hopi, but he had turned away and was staring out towards the river.

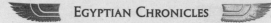

Why does he still look so cross? Isis wondered.

But now the priests were coming. The chief priest walked ahead, while the three others followed, carrying platters of meat on their heads and chanting prayers.

Hat-Neb drew Isis to his side. 'Stay close to me,' he instructed her. 'I'll keep you perfectly safe.'

Isis did as he said. With Hat-Neb's arm around her shoulder and the big fan-bearer just behind, she felt secure – which was just as well, because the surface of the pond was no longer still. Two sets of nostrils appeared, poking out of the water. They were followed by four golden eyes and huge log-like bodies. Isis felt her knees tremble.

The priests stood in a row and lifted the platters from their heads. The chief priest took a chunk of meat. The water in the pond was beginning to churn, and now two enormous heads rose out of it, their jaws opening to reveal rows of terrifying teeth.

Isis screamed. She couldn't help it. Hat-Neb's hand gripped her shoulder, and she gulped for air. Then she put her hands up to her face and peeped at the scene through her fingers. The chief priest threw the chunk of meat, and the jaws opened even wider. Tails thrashed the water as the first crocodile caught the meat and tossed it into its mouth with a few powerful snaps. The priest reached for more meat and threw it to the other crocodile, then kept on throwing until the platters were empty.

The priests resumed their chanting. Solemnly, they turned away from the pond and passed the spectators to walk slowly back towards the shrine. Isis knew they had to complete the ritual inside, away from public eyes. They would have saved some of the meat to present to the statue of the god, before sharing it among themselves.

The crocodiles were sinking back into the water. Soon, Isis could see nothing but nostrils and the ridges along their backs. Then the sacred pond was still again.

'There. Sobek is pleased,' murmured Hat-Neb. 'We have his blessing, little Isis.'

Isis let her hands slip down from her face, and took a deep breath. She had not been so close to crocodiles since the day her parents had died. But she had survived. She stared at the still water, and realised that her knees had stopped trembling.

Hopi trailed after the group as it headed back towards the shrine, dragging his feet. The whole event had upset him deeply, and he wasn't even sure why. Of course he was happy for Isis to overcome her fear of crocodiles – if, indeed, the sacrifice had worked. But he hated it being because of Hat-Neb. That was all wrong – just because he was rich, and could afford to squander his wealth on lambs like that . . .

Not squander, he told himself. If it had helped Isis, then it wasn't squandering. But all the same, Hopi resented it. Their father's last words had seared themselves on to his mind: *Look after Isis* . . . And Hopi had hoped to do just that. He'd hoped that one day, *he* would be the one to help Isis conquer her fears. And now this man Hat-Neb had swept into their lives and tucked his sister under his own big, fat arm.

What was worse, Hat-Neb seemed to have taken a dislike to Hopi. As they had approached the shrine, Hopi had heard him mutter into his fan-bearer's ear.

'Keep an eye on that boy,' he'd said.

So he, Hopi, was *that boy*. The fan-bearer had taken his master's word seriously. It wasn't just *an eye* that he was keeping on Hopi – he seemed to have at least four of them. Hopi felt watched the whole time, and he hated it. It gave him the creeps.

Isis looked up at the beautiful boat. This was not a fragile craft made of papyrus, or even a wobbly ferry. It was a big, solid boat that sat high out of the water.

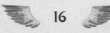

'You will be safe, Isis.' It was Sheri who spoke. She pointed up at the boat's cabin. 'Look. Hat-Neb is waiting for us. Come.'

Isis gazed up at the cabin. Hat-Neb was holding something in his arms, something small and furry. It was a cat. The sight of the little creature gave a final boost to her courage. Hat-Neb had done so much to help her, and it filled her with gladness to see him holding and stroking a cat. She took Sheri's hand on her left and Kia's hand on her right, and walked up to the boat's ladder. Bravely, without looking down, she clambered up to the deck.

'Welcome aboard!' Hat-Neb greeted her. 'And meet Killer, my most prized hunting cat.'

Killer was a sleek tabby with clear green eyes. Tentatively, Isis reached out to stroke and tickle him behind the ears, and he purred gratefully.

She smiled. 'We'll be friends,' she said.

'Better than that,' said Hat-Neb. 'We shall take him hunting, and you will see him track down the birds in the marshes.'

Isis had heard many tales of hunting in the marshes and the cleverness of the hunting cats. But she had never actually seen it for herself.

'May I hold him?' she asked.

Hat-Neb placed the cat in her arms. Killer wriggled

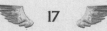

at first, but Isis held him firmly and carried on
stroking him until he relaxed. Together they watched
as Mut came aboard, followed by their luggage –
Sheri and Kia's lyres, lutes and flutes, along with their
wigs, gowns and make-up, plus mats and covers for
the cool nights that they would spend along the riverbank. She buried her cheek in Killer's soft fur. In spite
of everything, the trip would be a success.

But for Hopi, the trip had not yet begun. He was still
ten paces away from the boat, out of sight of the deck,
with the fan-bearer leaning over him.

'Empty it. Everything,' ordered the fan-bearer. He
was Nubian, with a heavy southern accent.

Silently, Hopi took the last items out of his linen
bag, then shook it upside down to show that there
was nothing left. The fan-bearer fingered his belongings, examining each of them closely.

'What is this?' The man held up a flat piece of limestone with hieroglyphs scribbled over it.

'What d'you think it is?' asked Hopi impatiently. It
was perfectly obvious.

The man towered over Hopi menacingly. 'It is a
rock. A rock is dangerous,' he said.

Hopi refused to be intimidated. 'Can't you see it's
for writing on?'

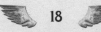

'All I see is that it is dangerous,' repeated the fan-bearer. 'This does not come on the boat.' And he threw the ostracon into a pile of dried-out palm fronds along the shore.

'Hey!' Hopi was furious, but the fan-bearer ignored him, and bent down to sift through the rest of Hopi's belongings.

'This,' said the man, picking up a papyrus basket. He pulled off the closely fitting lid, and peered inside. The basket was empty. 'Why you need this?'

Hopi was silent. The basket was one of his most treasured possessions, for he used it to house any snakes or scorpions that he caught. But he knew he mustn't say so.

'Well?' The fan-bearer was staring at him.

'It's my basket,' muttered Hopi.

'I see it is basket.'

'I . . . I put flowers in it. Flowers, reeds – stuff from the fields.' Hopi met the fan-bearer's gaze defiantly.

The man shrugged and gave a pitying smile. He put the basket down. It was the last item, and he waved his arm, indicating that Hopi could repack his linen bag. But then he caught sight of the stick in Hopi's right hand.

'Stick. This is dangerous,' he exclaimed, and reached out for it.

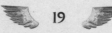

'No!' Hopi snatched it out of his way. 'I need it.'

'This is boat trip. No need for stick,' scoffed the fan-bearer.

But Hopi was determined. The stick had a fork at one end, which was essential for catching and handling snakes. He wasn't going anywhere without it. He thought quickly, then pointed down at his leg with its deep, jagged scars.

'Look at my leg. I can't manage without my stick,' he insisted. The row of crocodile scars was impressive.

The fan-bearer narrowed his eyes, then nodded. 'You pack your bag. Hurry. We are very soon leaving.'

Hopi bent to do as he said, placing his belongings one by one into his bag. He kept his features still, so that the fan-bearer could not see what he was feeling. But in his heart a cold fury was building.

 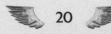

CHAPTER TWO

With the wind in its sails, the boat sailed south, against the flow of the Nile. Isis settled into the central cabin, where there were lots of comfortable cushions to sit on. It was cool, too, the wooden sides providing constant shade from the sun. While Sheri and Kia tuned their instruments and began to play some gentle melodies for Hat-Neb, a thin, serious-looking man appeared with some bottles of ointment to apply to his master's back.

Isis and Mut played with Killer, teasing him with a piece of cloth. Time and time again the cat pounced, his eyes wild, until at last he grew bored. He sat and licked his paws, then sauntered off to stretch out on a cushion. As the afternoon wore on, everyone became drowsy. The ointment man went out on to the deck. Hat-Neb fell asleep and began snoring in one corner,

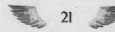 21

so Sheri and Kia laid down their instruments. Soon they were dozing, too. Only Mut and Isis remained awake, under the watchful gaze of the fan-bearer. Mut curled up on a cushion next to Killer and stroked him.

Isis sidled over to the fan-bearer. He shifted, but said nothing. Isis took in his enormous muscles and big, wide shoulders.

'What's your name?' she whispered.

The fan-bearer still said nothing.

Hat-Neb gave a particularly long, burbling snore, and Isis giggled. She was feeling mischievous. She put her face close to the Nubian's, and looked into his dark eyes.

'Are you allowed to laugh?' she enquired. She scrunched up her nose with her finger. Then she put her two little fingers in her mouth and stretched it wide. The Nubian's eyes slid away from hers, refusing to watch.

'Oh come *on*,' protested Isis. 'It's perfectly safe. You can talk to me.' She glanced at Mut, but she wasn't listening. Isis stuck her tongue out, then looped it right around until it touched the tip of her nose. 'I bet you can't do that,' she said. 'Not many people can.'

The faintest glimmer of a smile appeared on the

fan-bearer's face. Isis grinned. She was getting through to him!

'My name's Isis,' she told him. 'Go on, tell me yours.'

The muscles of the Nubian's cheeks began to move. Isis saw his hesitation and naughtily pinched his arm. His eyes flew wide open in protest.

'My name is Nebo,' he said in a deep voice. He rubbed his arm. 'And you are very bad girl.'

'Sorry.' Isis giggled again. 'It didn't *really* hurt, though, did it?'

Nebo shook his head, the faint smile quivering again. 'You are cheeky. Just like –' he began.

'Like who?'

The smile disappeared. Nebo looked away. 'No one,' he said.

But Isis was curious. 'Tell me,' she said. She decided to guess. 'Do *you* have a little girl somewhere? I bet you do.'

The fan-bearer stiffened. He was silent for a moment.

'Did something happen to her?' Isis knew she should leave it, but she couldn't resist.

Then Nebo looked directly at her and said, very quietly, 'This not something to talk about, Isis.'

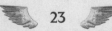

Isis looked back at him, and saw the suffering deep in his eyes. 'Sorry,' she said again. And this time, she meant it.

Hopi sat at the prow of the boat in the open-sided shelter. He had no desire to sit in the cabin with everyone else, especially after being so humiliated by the fan-bearer. Besides, it was much better out on the deck, where he could watch the crew and see the view to the riverbanks.

The crew made him curious. He would have expected an important man like Hat-Neb to employ Egypt's best sailors, but these men looked very rough and ready. They were not even Egyptian. They were all foreigners – hired sailors from somewhere far to the north. And they clearly hadn't been in the country long, because only their captain, Kerem, could speak Egyptian. The rest spoke a strange language that Hopi had never heard before.

The boat was gliding slowly up the river, passing palm trees and open fields, where the barley and flax swayed in the breeze. Hopi waved to farm labourers and children, laundrymen pounding linen on the rocks, and fishermen in their little papyrus boats. Sometimes, he saw evidence of crocodiles: the ripple of a snout in the shallows, or a grey-brown body basking in the sun.

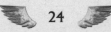

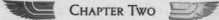

'Young Hopi! You're sitting comfortably, I see,' said Tutmose, appearing from across the deck. He sat down cross-legged in the shelter, wiping his hands on a piece of linen.

'I like it better here than in the cabin.'

'You avoid the company of others?'

Hopi hesitated. He wanted Tutmose to think well of him. 'Not always. There is a right time for everything.'

'Wise words,' said Tutmose. 'But then, you're obviously a very wise young man.'

'Oh, I don't know about that,' said Hopi.

'A trainee priest of Serqet? Don't be modest,' said Tutmose. 'Only a few are chosen for such a role. You're one of a small elite, you must know that!'

Hopi felt a flush of pride, mixed with embarrassment. He had received very little praise in his life. Only a few weeks ago, he had been a nobody.

'But I know very little,' he said. 'I am only at the beginning of my apprenticeship.'

'But you know a fair bit about snakes, I suppose? You've handled them, and so on?'

'Oh yes! Of course.' That was the one thing that Hopi knew he was good at.

'So, there you are!' exclaimed Tutmose. 'A special gift indeed. Most people shrink in terror from doing such a thing.'

'Yes, I suppose so.' Hopi had to agree. 'But you're a doctor. You must know a lot about them, too.'

Tutmose shook his head. 'I spend all my time flattering men like Hat-Neb. I offered my services because I heard that he suffers with his back. Today I have been applying ointments to it, but there is really nothing wrong. He is the sort of man who creates imaginary ailments, but chooses to ignore any real ones.' He shrugged dismissively. 'I have little opportunity to learn new things. I would be glad to discover anything that you can teach me.'

Hopi could hardly believe it. A royal doctor, wanting to learn from *him*! It certainly made up for being treated like a criminal by Hat-Neb and his guard.

He smiled. 'I'd be happy to, sir.'

'And you must let me know if there is anything I can do in return.'

It was a generous offer, but Hopi could think of nothing, for the moment. 'I certainly will do that, sir.'

They lapsed into silence. Hopi blessed his good fortune – this trip would be insufferable without Tutmose. He flushed with anger once more as he thought of how the fan-bearer had gone through his things. He wondered what the doctor would say, if he knew.

'Perhaps you could tell me,' he said, 'the name of

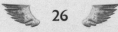

Hat-Neb's fan-bearer?'

Tutmose looked at him quickly. 'Hat-Neb's . . . you mean the Nubian? Nebo?'

'Yes. You say Nebo is his name?'

Tutmose nodded, then glanced over his shoulder to check that no one was listening. He moved a little closer. 'Take care, young Hopi,' he said in a low voice. 'That guard is a dangerous man.'

'I know,' said Hopi.

Tutmose shuffled closer and placed a hand on Hopi's arm. 'Let me give you some advice, my young friend,' he said.

Hopi nodded. 'I'll be happy to hear it.'

'Make sure you keep your knowledge to yourself. The Nubian says little, but hears much. He hunts out the slightest threat to his master and squashes it like a mosquito under his thumb. Do not raise suspicion by revealing your skills.'

So Tutmose didn't trust him, either. Hopi was glad. 'I wasn't going to,' he said. 'I'll avoid him as much as I can.'

Tutmose sat back again, and nodded. 'Very wise.'

Isis poked her head out of the cabin. She was beginning to wonder what had become of Hopi; he hadn't joined them once since boarding the boat. In fact, he'd

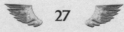

looked gloomy ever since Hat-Neb had first come to visit. It was time to investigate. Outside on the deck, the afternoon sunlight was becoming golden and mellow. Isis found Hopi in the shelter at the front of the boat, deep in conversation with the ointment man. He looked up as she approached.

'Isis, have you met Tutmose?' he asked her. 'He's a doctor. A royal doctor. He has worked in the king's court.'

'I've just seen him treating Hat-Neb.' Isis sat down next to her brother to study the doctor more closely. He was thin, with long, nervous hands; his small, beady eyes were set deep into their sockets, and darted to and fro as he spoke. 'What were you putting on Hat-Neb's back?' she asked. 'Is he sick?'

Tutmose smiled – a cold, humourless smile. 'You might say that he brings sickness on himself,' he said.

Isis was alarmed. 'How? What's wrong with him?'

The doctor shook his head. 'This is not your concern,' he said.

'But it is! I mean – I'd hate to think he was sick! He's being so kind to us,' insisted Isis. 'Can you cure him?'

The humourless smile appeared again. 'Of course.'

Isis stared at him. Something told her that he didn't care whether he cured Hat-Neb or not. It made her angry. 'So, can you cure Hopi's limp?' she challenged him.

Tutmose looked affronted. 'I do not give cures for wounds that have already healed,' he said.

'But it hasn't healed. Not completely,' Isis goaded him. 'It still hurts sometimes, doesn't it, Hopi? And you still limp.'

Hopi glared at her. 'My leg's as good as it will ever get. You know that, Isis.'

Isis shrugged. 'I would have thought a royal doctor could cure anything.'

'I'm sure he can cure most things,' said Hopi.

Isis met his gaze, and saw that her brother's eyes were flashing. He was annoyed with her and she felt indignant. Hopi was supposed to be on *her* side. She wanted to talk to him on his own, but Tutmose showed no sign of moving. Instead, the doctor leaned forward and smiled.

'Is that the first time you have seen a doctor at work, Isis?' he asked, placing a bony finger on her hand.

Isis snatched her hand away. 'Of course it isn't,' she said. 'Who do you think treated Hopi?' She had been young at the time, but she had a very clear memory of the doctors who had tended Hopi's leg. They had been kind to treat him at all, for there had been little

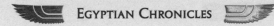

inheritance to pay them with.

'Not a good memory, perhaps,' said Tutmose.

'No, it isn't,' said Isis. She wished she'd never started talking about it.

'It was a difficult time for us both. Isis has been terrified of crocodiles ever since,' put in Hopi.

That smile curled the doctor's lips again. 'Ah, now there's an ailment I've never had to treat!' he exclaimed.

Isis glared at him and scrambled back to her feet. 'Well, Hat-Neb *has* treated it!' she snapped. 'That makes him much more of a doctor than *you* are, doesn't it?' And she spun round and flounced along the deck.

Hopi was astonished. He had never seen Isis behave that way. He felt embarrassed. Of course, Tutmose could have been a little more sensitive; his sister's fear of crocodiles had been very real before the offerings to Sobek. But Isis had been rude from the start.

Tutmose raised an eyebrow. 'Quite fiery, your little sister,' he remarked.

'Well, she can be,' Hopi admitted. 'I'm sorry. I'll make sure she apologises right away.' He began to get up. 'I'll go after her –'

Tutmose placed a hand on his shoulder. 'No, no,

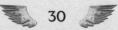

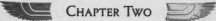

there's no need,' he said. 'Girls are governed by strange impulses. I have seen worse cases than this.'

Hopi settled down again, feeling torn. He didn't want to offend this man. There seemed to be so much that they could gain from each other.

'Well, thank you for understanding,' he said.

'Not at all, not at all,' said Tutmose. He got to his feet. 'Now, I'm just going to check my list of supplies. We will be stopping at some useful villages – places where certain herbs grow, and so on. I hope to do some stocking up. You will excuse me.'

'Of course.'

Hopi would have liked to see what supplies he was talking about, but he didn't feel he could ask just yet. Still, there was time. In spite of Hat-Neb and Nebo, and in spite of this strange behaviour from Isis, he was enjoying himself. He had rarely met anyone who would talk to him the way Tutmose did – apart, of course, from Menna. Few people were interested in the lives and habits of desert creatures, yet this doctor seemed to have nothing but respect for his knowledge.

He thought for a moment about Isis. He really ought to try to talk to her about the way she had spoken to Tutmose. It was too bad. But now she was in the cabin with Hat-Neb, and Hopi was reluctant to

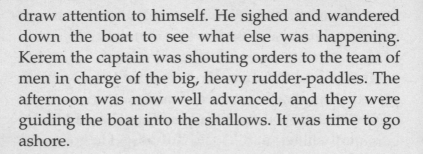

draw attention to himself. He sighed and wandered down the boat to see what else was happening. Kerem the captain was shouting orders to the team of men in charge of the big, heavy rudder-paddles. The afternoon was now well advanced, and they were guiding the boat into the shallows. It was time to go ashore.

On the riverbank, Hat-Neb sent Kerem with members of the crew to buy fresh poultry and fish, along with vegetables, herbs and beans from the nearby village gardens. Mats were unrolled under palm trees, and a little camp was set up for the night.

'Now, my daughters,' said Hat-Neb, coming up to Isis and Mut. 'It is almost time for you to show me how well you can perform. And just to make you dance that little bit better, I have something to give to you.' From behind his back, he produced a little casket, and opened the lid. 'Look.'

Isis and Mut peered inside and gasped. There lay two beautiful bead collars, each with a scarab amulet embedded in the middle.

'Are these really for us?' asked Mut.

'Just for you. One each. Would you like to try them on?'

Hat-Neb reached into the casket himself, and

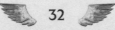

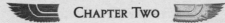

gently lifted the first collar out. It had three rows of carnelian beads, and the scarab was finely carved out of turquoise. It was exquisite.

'Come, Isis. This one is for you,' said Hat-Neb. He placed the collar around her neck and fastened the clasp. Isis felt the unfamiliar beadwork with her fingers and smiled. She had never owned anything so lovely in her life.

Hat-Neb did the same for Mut, then sent them off to show Sheri and Kia. The two women exclaimed in admiration as the two girls twirled around.

'Now you must take them off and keep them very safe,' said Kia. 'It's time to get ready for dancing. You can put them on again later.'

The sun set over the palm trees to the west, on the other side of the river, and fires were lit in the camp. As the crew cook prepared the food, Sheri and Kia reached for their instruments, and Isis and Mut began to dance. Isis felt a thrill of happiness and freedom as she twirled around, stepping in perfect time with Mut. Most of the parties they worked at were in people's houses and courtyards, where there was not very much space. Here, there was the whole riverbank. They performed their best acrobatics – frontflips and backflips, several in a row; cartwheels; somersaults. With every turn, Hat-Neb roared his

approval. At last they stopped, and bowed to their employer.

'Wonderful,' he enthused. 'Now, let us all eat. Later, you can dance again.'

Isis sat down next to Sheri.

'No, no, come and sit here, my daughters,' exclaimed Hat-Neb. 'You and Mut must eat the choicest fish and meat. I will select it for you myself.'

As Isis accepted a tender piece of goose meat, she looked across the fire and saw that Hopi was still talking to that horrible doctor. It bothered her. Couldn't her brother see what he was really like?

Perhaps he *would* see, after a few days. And meanwhile, she would try not to worry. Meeting Hat-Neb was one of the best things that had ever happened to her, almost like finding the father she had lost. Maybe Hopi would come to feel the same way, in time.

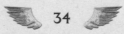

CHAPTER THREE

Isis woke up with a start. Something had disturbed her, outside the light fabric shelter where she and Mut lay with Sheri and Kia. She sat up and listened. Perhaps it was nothing, just the breeze in the palm trees. But she was about to lie down again when she saw a human shape, silhouetted against the fabric by the moonlight. There was definitely someone there.

Her heart thudding a little faster, Isis got to her feet and tiptoed outside. The palm trees rustled and swayed, and she slipped behind one of the straight, tall trunks.

The camp was silent, so quiet that Isis could hear the lap-lap of the River Nile against the banks. She peered out from around the tree. Next to their shelter were two smaller ones for Tutmose and Hopi, and then, slightly apart, was a bigger shelter for Hat-Neb.

 35

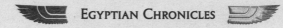

Some of the crew stood guard around it, dozing, while the solid form of Nebo lay across the entrance.

She began to think she must have imagined the shadow. The night air was cool, giving her goose-pimples, and she decided to head back to bed. Then something caught her eye, down towards the river. Hurriedly, she ducked back behind the trunk and watched.

It was Tutmose, creeping stealthily from the direction of the boat.

Huh, thought Isis. She wasn't surprised. Who else would be creeping around suspiciously late at night? He was carrying something long and thin. Isis stared, trying to make out what it was. Tutmose turned it slightly, so that she saw it more fully. It was Hat-Neb's ostrich-feather fan.

Silently, Tutmose stepped inside his shelter and disappeared. Isis stood rooted to the spot for a few seconds. Was Hopi awake? Did he know about the strange behaviour of his 'friend', the doctor? She pursed her lips. She'd known there was something slippery about him. She went back to bed, her mind made up. In the morning, she'd warn her brother – first thing.

Not long after dawn, Isis crept outside to see the boat crew already bustling about, preparing breakfast

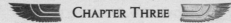

and carrying things back down to the riverside. Mut was still fast asleep. Now, she decided, was her chance to speak to Hopi. She pulled on her linen gown and ran to the back of her brother's shelter. Peeping underneath the fabric, she saw that Hopi was still asleep. She wriggled inside.

'Hopi!' She shook her brother's shoulder.

'Wh-what?' he mumbled sleepily.

'Wake up. I need to speak to you.'

Hopi rolled over and opened his eyes. 'Isis.' He frowned, and closed his eyes again.

She sat down next to him. 'Hopi, you have to listen to me,' she said urgently. 'You must be careful. I know Tutmose is up to something. I know he is . . . are you listening to me?' She shook his shoulder again.

'Stop it!' Hopi shrugged her off irritably. He sat up and wiped his hand over his face. Isis waited for a moment, letting him get his bearings. 'So. What is it?' he asked eventually.

'It's Tutmose. He creeps around the camp at night, stealing things from the boat – things belonging to Hat-Neb. I saw him carrying his fan, you know, the one that Nebo carries! He's horrible, Hopi –'

'Don't be stupid, Isis. You don't know what you're talking about.' Hopi cut her short. He flung off his covers and stood up. 'I don't know what's happened

to you. Yesterday you were very rude to Tutmose. You didn't apologise and then you didn't speak to me all evening. So what's going on?'

Isis felt a pang of shame. 'I'm sorry about that,' she said. 'I was busy with Hat-Neb.'

'Hat-Neb, Hat-Neb!' exclaimed Hopi. 'You think he's wonderful, don't you? All he does is flatter you and give you things, and try to make you believe he's so very, very nice –'

'Well, he *is*.'

'No, he isn't.'

Isis was shocked. How could her brother say such a thing? 'He's one of the nicest people I've ever met!' she declared. 'He says I'm just like a daughter to him.'

'Isis!' Hopi sounded really angry. 'You've only just met this man. He is *not* your father. He is nothing like your father. Don't you ever, ever dare say that again.'

'But he protects me and cares for me,' pouted Isis. She was upset. Why couldn't Hopi see how good Hat-Neb was? 'And he's cured my fear of crocodiles.'

Hopi opened his mouth to say something, then snapped it shut again. He ran a hand through his hair. Then he stood in front of Isis and placed his hands on his hips. 'Hat-Neb is rich, it is true. But only Sobek himself could have cured your fear,' he said. 'And I don't want to hear any more of this nonsense about

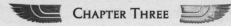

Tutmose. He's a doctor, with important work to do.'

'But I saw him –'

Hopi swept his hand around the shelter. 'Think, Isis. We're in the middle of nowhere. This shelter, and your shelter, and the shelter that Tutmose slept in are all going back on to the boat. There will be nothing left on the riverbank. So how can he possibly have stolen something? He'd have to take it straight back on to the boat again, wouldn't he?'

Isis didn't know what to say. Hopi's words made sense. She hated arguing with him, but she couldn't agree with him over Hat-Neb. And even if Tutmose hadn't been stealing, she still thought that what she had seen was very strange.

Hopi watched as Hat-Neb strode up and down the deck, giving Kerem his orders. As usual, Nebo stood just behind him, holding the ostrich-feather fan firmly in his grip. A fan was a magical object, a symbol of life-giving breath. Hopi smiled to himself. Hat-Neb's fan was still very much where it should be. Isis must have been imagining things.

The wind that usually blew from the north was dropping. The crew clambered around the sails, but it was no use. The boat was drifting slowly to a halt. Hat-Neb was annoyed, but this wasn't a rowing boat.

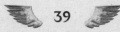

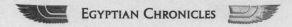

The crew had only one option – to steer the boat to the shore, and wait for the wind to pick up again.

Hopi was pleased. He knew the ways of the wind very well. It would stay calm through the heat of the day, and only get breezy again later in the afternoon. He had time to explore on his own, as he did when he was at home. This was a deserted stretch of river. Beyond a narrow strip of green, there was nothing but yellow rocks and sand: the perfect hunting ground for snakes. So, once on the shore, he slipped away, and began to climb a low, barren hill. From there, he would be able to survey all around.

The midday sun was hot. Noises carried on the still air, and Hopi could hear the shouts of the crew setting up shelters as he reached the brow of the hill. He turned to view the scene. The River Nile shimmered, a thick ribbon of calm, deep blue as far as he could see. It was unusually empty, as there were no villages nearby. Hat-Neb's boat was alone.

Hopi set off again, scanning the ground for telltale signs of life. Patches of sand drifted up against the rocks, and he looked at these particularly carefully. Eventually, he spotted what he'd hoped for: the squiggly track of a snake, repeated time and again as it sidewinded its way across the sand. He bent over to inspect it more closely. It was fresh. He could see the

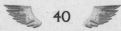

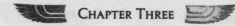

impression of the whole body, and knew at once that it was the trail of a horned viper.

He followed the trail until it disappeared, seemingly into nowhere. Then he squatted, quiet and still, as he often did, letting himself become part of the landscape. Beads of sweat began to run down his face, but he didn't move a muscle. A fly buzzed around his head. He ignored it. The only parts of him that moved were his eyes, which roved over the sand.

At last, his patience was rewarded. His eyes rested on two tiny horns, perfectly camouflaged. The horned viper preferred to hunt at night, when it was cooler; during the day, it buried itself, leaving just these little horns showing. Hopi gripped his stick tighter. Then, with a lightning move of his wrist, he flicked the stick so that its fork landed just behind the horns, pinning the viper down. The whole of its body emerged from the sand at once, thrashing in protest. It was a beauty. Grinning in delight, Hopi scrambled to his feet. With his free hand he opened his papyrus basket, and whipped the snake into it. Quickly, he fitted the lid.

Brushing himself down, Hopi wondered how long he had been gone. He squinted up at the sun and saw that it had begun to move to the west. He should hurry. He hitched the bag on to his shoulder and set off, feeling very proud of himself. This would be the

perfect start to explaining his work to Tutmose. He had walked further than he thought, and began to half-run, half-limp, worried that the boat might leave without him. The river came into view, and Hat-Neb's little camp, still resting on the riverbank. Hopi stopped. Hat-Neb's boat was no longer alone. There was another, advancing from the south. And it was huge.

The massive wooden barge was laden with a great stone obelisk of pure granite that looked golden in the light of the sun, and a row of solid limestone blocks. It was so big that it had to be pulled along by a tug boat manned by twelve strong rowers. Hopi watched it advance slowly, surely up the river. He shaded his eyes from the sun and peered at the rowers. Was he imagining it, or was the barge slowing down?

He hurried on. Some of Hat-Neb's crew were standing on the riverbank, watching the rowers. There was no doubt about it now. The rowers were pulling in, tugging the massive barge after them. They were going to stop. Excited, Hopi began to limp as fast as he could towards the shore.

Isis heard shouts. The Nubian leaped to his feet, followed by Tutmose. Hat-Neb awoke from his slumber and sat up. Isis ran to join Nebo and the doctor at the

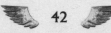

entrance of the shelter, but Nebo's heavy hand stopped her from going outside. She could just see Kerem, calling out to members of the crew.

'Is it pirates?' demanded Hat-Neb, still half asleep on some cushions.

'No, master,' said Nebo. 'A barge crew.'

'A barge crew!' Hat-Neb sat up, fully alert. 'What's their cargo?'

'A consignment of stone from the quarries of the south, by the looks of it,' said Tutmose. 'An obelisk, and about twenty blocks.'

Hat-Neb slumped back down again and closed his eyes. 'Well, they won't be able to stop,' he murmured. 'What are the crew getting excited about?'

'Actually,' said Tutmose, 'they *are* stopping. It would seem they have recognised the insignia on your boat.'

Hat-Neb's eyes flew open again. He stared at Nebo. Then, with a great deal of effort, he got to his feet.

'You must leave,' said Tutmose. 'At once. I will go and talk to them.'

'No,' growled Nebo. 'I go.'

Isis stared at the three men. Mut joined her and they held hands, frightened and bewildered. Sheri and Kia rose from their cushions and put their

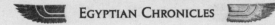

arms around the girls.

'If you go to meet them, you will make it worse,' insisted Tutmose. 'I will speak to them. I will tell them you are not on board. Take the women and children, and hide in the desert until they have gone.'

Isis was baffled. Who were these men? And why should Hat-Neb have to hide from them? Then her thoughts flew to Hopi. She'd seen him walking up the hill. She hoped he wouldn't get muddled up with all of this.

Nebo was clearly furious. 'This is my work. The crew – they will do nothing.'

'Don't be ridiculous. You're wasting time. The crew have a great deal to lose and they will do as I say.' Tutmose peered out of the tent. 'Hurry. They are coming ashore.'

Hat-Neb was sweating. 'He's right,' he muttered. 'Come, Nebo. We must go.'

The Nubian hesitated for only a second longer. As more shouts reached their ears, he turned to the women, his face still clouded with anger.

'You follow me,' he said, ushering Hat-Neb through a gap in the back of the tent, through a small clump of doum palms and away from the sounds of shouting.

He marched quickly, glancing back to check that

everyone was keeping up. Hat-Neb puffed and panted, his arms flapping by the sides of his flabby body.

They reached the edge of the vegetation, but the Nubian kept walking, out into the scorching desert. The sun was beating down, the rocks shimmering with heat. Eventually, he stopped behind some yellow boulders.

'We stay here,' instructed Nebo.

There was a little bit of shade behind the biggest rock, and Hat-Neb flopped against it in relief.

'Oh! By Amun, I can't walk any further!' he exclaimed. His eyeliner was smudged, making black circles under his eyes, and sweat was streaked down his face. Sweat had soaked through his beautiful linen gown so that the pleats had almost disappeared. He leaned his head back against the rock and closed his eyes. 'Where's my fan?' he murmured. 'I need my fan.'

But Nebo ignored him. He had walked around the rocks to stare back the way they had come.

Isis crept to join him. 'Who are those men?' she whispered. 'You wanted to fight them yourself, didn't you?'

Nebo looked down at her briefly. 'I like to fight,' he said.

'You *like* it?'

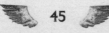

Nebo didn't respond. He stood perfectly still, listening. They could hear shouts in the distance, but they didn't seem to be getting any closer.

'When I am fighting, I am not thinking,' said the Nubian eventually, placing his hand on her shoulder.

'And that's why you like it?'

Nebo shrugged. 'Yes.'

Isis thought about it. 'Perhaps it's the same when I dance,' she said. 'Then I don't think about anything. I just *am*.'

'Then you understand this.'

'I think so.' Isis nodded gravely. 'You won't let those men hurt us, will you?'

Nebo's grip on her shoulder tightened. 'I am very strong, Isis. I keep you safe.'

Isis leaned against him. He felt solid, as though nothing could make him falter. And she believed him. Nothing could happen while he was guarding them. She just hoped that Hopi was not in danger, either.

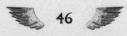

CHAPTER FOUR

Hopi stopped halfway down the barren hillside. There was no sign of Hat-Neb or Nebo; there was only Tutmose, beckoning to the crew. Hopi watched as the tug drew steadily closer. The barge was much too heavy to come to shore, so instead it was being anchored, and the tug cut loose. The twelve rowers were landing alone.

Hopi scrambled down the last stretch of hillside, ducked behind a few scrubby trees near the riverbank and crept along towards the rowers, who were pulling the tug into the shallows. He could hear them talking among themselves.

'This is the perfect opportunity,' said one. 'A quiet stretch of river. No one will ever know.'

'Yes,' agreed someone else. 'But we'll have to be quick.'

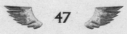

Another sounded more uneasy. 'I don't like the look of the crew,' he said. 'Who are they? They're not Egyptian.'

'That's a good thing,' said their leader. 'Who cares about them?'

They moved off up the bank. Peering through the shrubs, Hopi saw that Tutmose had led the crew to meet them. The two groups stopped, facing each other.

'Greetings, Senmut,' said Tutmose. 'This is an unexpected encounter.'

'Greetings,' said the man. 'Unexpected! Yes indeed. What a stroke of luck!'

'Ah, now there I cannot agree with you,' said Tutmose. 'I can guess what you have in mind, but this is neither the time nor the place.'

Senmut snorted. 'It is the ideal time and the ideal place!'

'Believe me,' said Tutmose, 'these men have been promised a fortune when we get to Djeba. They will not let you pass. You are making a mistake.'

'Enough talk!' cried one of the rowers. 'Let's just get on with it! Come on, men!'

There was a flash of metal as the rowers drew axes and daggers. Just as quickly, Hat-Neb's crew drew daggers, too. The two groups of men eyed each other,

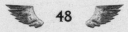

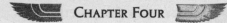

their bodies tense. Suddenly, one of the rowers leaped forward. Tutmose, unarmed, scuttled out of the way. The rower lunged with his axe, and slashed the arm of one of Hat-Neb's crew. The man gave a cry of rage as blood spurted out, and thrust his dagger wildly. All the men began to howl – great bloodthirsty yells – and threw themselves into battle.

Hopi was horrified. He had never seen anything like it. They would all kill each other! Already, blood was flowing. He tried to swallow, but his mouth was dry. What could he do? What could he do? He felt rooted to the spot, nothing but a useless cripple!

Then he had an idea. He ripped open his linen bag and pulled the lid off his basket, reached inside and grasped the viper behind its neck. Then he half-limped, half-ran out from behind the bushes.

'Stop this!' he screamed. 'Stop this violence! Or I will release this creature upon you!'

One by one, the men caught sight of the viper and recoiled in terror.

'A snake!' cried the rowers. 'A viper! It is Apep himself!'

Hat-Neb's crew called and jabbered to each other in their own language, backing away from Hopi, who waved the snake high in the air above his head.

'I am a priest of Serqet!' he cried, hardly knowing

what he was saying. 'The goddess will punish you! Shame, shame on you all!'

The men on both sides cowered, their eyes great pools of fear. Some of them began to groan, gripping the wounds they had received, blood seeping through their fingers. Then Tutmose, who had been skulking behind the crew, stepped forward and stood next to Hopi.

'The boy is right!' he said. 'See how the gods have come among us. The fighting must stop!' He turned to the rowers and raised his arms in the air. 'Return to your barge!' he ordered them. 'I told you that this is neither the time nor the place. Now you see that the gods agree with me!'

Senmut, their leader, gazed at Hopi. 'We can fight a crew of men,' he said, with awe in his voice, 'but we cannot fight the gods.'

Hopi was still holding the snake up high. Now, he lowered it slowly, and realised that he was shaking. He looked at the snake, with its cold yellow eyes, and silently thanked it. The man who had started the fighting stepped forward. He had a wound on his upper arm, from which blood was trickling, but he didn't seem to feel it.

'We shall go,' he said gruffly. 'But you must know the truth, Tutmose. This matter cannot rest.'

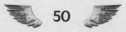

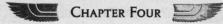

'I know,' said Tutmose. 'Believe me, I know.'

The man turned and started walking back towards the tug. 'And if that motley crew of yours think they'll get a fortune in Djeba, they are even more foolish than they look!' he shouted over his shoulder.

The sun on the yellow rocks was blinding.

'It's hot,' croaked Hat-Neb. 'So hot. I can't bear it . . . can't bear it.'

Isis was worried. Hat-Neb really seemed to be suffering. Yes, it was hot – but it was always hot in the afternoon.

'It's a pity we didn't bring any water,' said Sheri. 'But I suppose we had to leave in too much of a hurry for that.' She stepped forward and wiped Hat-Neb's brow with the loose end of her gown.

Nebo was still gazing out towards the river. The shouting had stopped. There was just the baking heat of the desert, and Hat-Neb's gasps and groans. Isis wondered if Hopi had seen what had happened. She desperately hoped he was safe.

At last, Nebo moved. 'We go,' he said.

But Isis wasn't sure that Hat-Neb *could* move. He seemed to have half-melted, half-slumped into the rock. Bravely, she took his arm.

'It's not far,' she whispered.

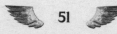

She felt the weight of him as Hat-Neb struggled upright, and smelt the pungent odour of his sweat. Yet his skin was strangely cold and clammy for someone so hot. Nebo took his arm on the other side, and the group set out. Hat-Neb walked with his eyes almost closed, leaning heavily on his fan-bearer's arm.

He is sick, thought Isis, *but he's too proud to admit to it. He needs a doctor.*

Everything seemed upside down. Tutmose the doctor had gone off with the crew, while Nebo the fighter had stayed here with them. Shouldn't it have been the other way round?

The rowers limped back to their tug boat, leaving a trail of blood behind them. None of them seemed mortally wounded, but all the same Hopi couldn't help wondering how they would manage to row their boat away.

He turned to Tutmose, and realised that the crew were rooted to the spot, staring at him. Of course: he was still holding the viper.

'I'd better let it loose,' he said.

Tutmose shook his head vehemently. 'I can't allow that.'

'But the men are afraid,' said Hopi.

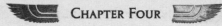

'Don't you see?' Tutmose raised his hand towards the sky. 'This is no mere viper! As far as these men are concerned, the gods themselves came among us!'

Hopi looked down at the snake. He had meant to show it to Tutmose, of course. But he had hoped they could keep it a secret. Now that the crew knew all about it, things were very different. Someone might be tempted to disturb it. It might strike. A bite from a horned viper might not kill a strong man, but it would make him very sick. Without Menna's spells and potions close by, Hopi wasn't sure he could offer treatment.

'You *must* keep it,' hissed Tutmose into his ear, 'or the men will cease to believe that the gods have saved them.'

Hopi looked at the faces of the men. None of them seemed to know what to do. Even their leader, Kerem, looked confused.

'This is the meaning of power,' Tutmose told Hopi. 'It is knowing that others fear you. As a priest, this is a lesson you must learn. Let us keep the snake with us. We may yet need it again.'

His words puzzled Hopi. What did he mean, *need it again*? He didn't want power over the men. Nevertheless, the snake may have saved several lives. The thought gave him a strange sense of pride.

Slowly, he walked back to the place where he had dropped his bag, and lowered the snake into his papyrus basket.

Tutmose turned to Kerem. 'You must return to the boat,' he told him. 'The gods of Egypt rose up to protect you. Make sure your men understand this. And let them know that we have a great and powerful priest on board.' He paused. 'But say nothing of the snake to Hat-Neb and Nebo. Let them think that you fought for them bravely. I am sure you understand why.'

'I understand,' said Kerem. 'I will tell the men.'

Then Tutmose turned to Hopi. 'There, young priest,' he said. 'The crew will say nothing, and it would be best for everyone if we do the same, don't you think?'

All was quiet back on the shore. The camp had been packed away. Isis looked up at the boat deck and saw that the crew were already on board. She felt a sudden stab of panic about Hopi. What if he hadn't come back?

Painfully, gasping with every step, Hat-Neb climbed up the boat ladder. Isis followed just behind him, anxious to see if her brother was on board. But the first thing she saw was blood. Blood on men's

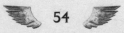

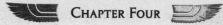

arms and faces. Drips of blood across the deck of the boat. Blood on the tip of a dagger that a man still held in his hand. She went cold.

No one spoke as Hat-Neb staggered across the deck, his eyes glazed. He barely seemed to notice the crew or their injuries. He made straight for the cool shade of the cabin without a backward glance. Isis looked around, horrified. Tutmose was working hard, bandaging wounds with swathes of linen. And then she saw Hopi, carrying some fresh bandages from the cabin.

'You're safe!' she exclaimed, rushing across the deck to greet him.

'Yes, I'm fine.' Hopi bent down to give Tutmose the bandages.

As he straightened up again, Isis pulled him to one side. 'So what happened?' she whispered.

'The boat was attacked,' said Hopi. 'But it's all over now.'

'But who were they? Did you see what happened?' insisted Isis.

Her brother wouldn't give her an answer. 'Keep your voice down, Isis,' he muttered, glancing around the deck.

Isis felt hurt. She was usually the first person that Hopi would talk to. She pursed her lips. 'Hat-Neb was very sick in the desert,' she announced in a loud

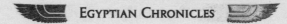

voice. 'Tutmose should go and see to him at once.'

Tutmose turned around from bandaging a man's arm, piercing Isis with his dark, beady eyes. 'And who are you to say what I should or should not do?'

'These men are not as important as Hat-Neb,' retorted Isis.

'That's hardly for you to say,' snapped Tutmose.

The man gave a yelp of pain as the bandage shifted, and Tutmose turned back to his patient. Isis looked at Hopi, and saw that she had made him angry again.

Oh no, she thought. *And all because of that sneaky, horrible doctor!*

It was unbearable. She spun on her heel and ran into the cabin.

Inside, Hat-Neb was spreadeagled on his cushions. Sheri and Kia were wiping his forehead while Mut hovered, looking helpless.

'Food,' he gasped. 'I need food.' He gestured towards one of the cabin caskets. 'Honey pastries. Dates. Dried figs. Something sweet.'

Kia opened the casket. Isis and Mut peered inside. It was stuffed with the finest dried fruits and delicacies. Kia lifted out a honey-coated pastry and placed it in a bowl with a handful of fat, golden dates. Hat-Neb reached for them in relief and ate hungrily,

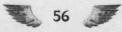

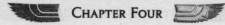

closing his eyes with pleasure.

'Wine,' he murmured.

Sheri reached for the flagon that rested in one corner, and poured Hat-Neb a gobletful. He downed the wine in just a few gulps, and held out the goblet for more.

'Much better,' he announced, smacking his lips. 'Now, Nebo, where's Tutmose?'

Isis was pleased. The doctor would *have* to see to Hat-Neb now. After a few moments, the flap of the cabin swung open, and Tutmose stepped in.

Hat-Neb grunted. 'I await your report.'

'Indeed,' nodded Tutmose. 'None are too badly hurt. But I hear that you were taken unwell in the desert. The heat, perhaps. Is this true?'

'Me?' Hat-Neb looked offended. 'I grew up in the desert. The gods made me strong as an ox. I can cope with it perfectly well.'

A faint smile curved the doctor's thin lips, and he slid a mean look at Isis. 'I am glad to hear it.'

Isis felt her cheeks flush. But she was puzzled, too. It was clear that Hat-Neb *was* sick, however hard he tried to deny it. Yet surely Tutmose could see the truth. What kind of a doctor was he if he couldn't?

Hat-Neb sat up and belched, then reached for another date. 'Bunch of troublemakers, was it?

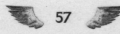

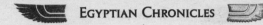

Anyone you know?'

'No, I was wrong there – total strangers, I'm glad to say. A maverick crew from the quarries. You know how they make use of criminals.'

'Yes, yes. And the crew fought them off?' Hat-Neb was stroking his chin.

'That's right. They are fierce fighters.' Tutmose nodded. 'Very fierce.'

'Good, good,' said Hat-Neb dismissively. 'Well, that's that. My back feels in need of a massage. Rub some of those ointments on it, would you?'

That evening, camp was in a little date-palm grove set back from the riverbank. It was a cool, dim place with dry palm fronds strewn on the ground and a thick cover of fresh ones overhead. While the crew unloaded, Sheri and Kia disappeared between the trees with Isis and Mut; Tutmose helped Hat-Neb to shore, and led him to rest.

Hopi lingered on the deck for a while, keen to keep in the background. The crew worked slowly. Hopi noticed that they were trying to compensate for the two most badly hurt, who could not carry heavy loads. Nebo appeared on the shore, watching their progress. And then, suddenly, he grabbed one of the injured men.

'Open your mouth,' he ordered, making signs to show what he meant.

The man did as he said.

'You drink wine.'

The man could not speak Egyptian. He said nothing, but pointed to the wound on his shoulder. The rest of the crew stopped working to watch.

Nebo shook the man hard. 'You steal wine from the hold.'

Kerem tried to intervene. 'The men are in pain,' he said. 'They can't work without –'

'You their leader,' Nebo interrupted him. 'I show you how you treat men who steal.' And he landed a heavy punch into the injured man's stomach.

Hopi was appalled. He stepped into the shadow of the cabin as the man collapsed to his knees, coughing and retching.

'Get up,' ordered Nebo. 'Or I do it again.'

The rest of the crew looked angry and sullen as the man struggled to his feet. Silently, he shouldered the mats that he had been carrying, and staggered off towards the camp.

'Tell your men to work faster,' Nebo ordered Kerem. 'The sun will soon set.' And he marched through the date palms back to his master.

Hopi felt shaken. He wasn't at all surprised, but

Nebo's actions had sickened him, just the same. He sat and stared at his hands, trying to forget the way the man had crumpled to the ground.

Hat-Neb drank heavily that night. Hopi noticed the crew watching him with resentment as they ate their meagre rations. Hat-Neb glugged his flagon, pouring goblet after goblet, urging on his performers with whoops and loud applause. Isis and Mut danced and danced, twirling in the firelight, while Sheri and Kia played every tune they knew, then played them all again.

'Bravo, bravo!' cried Hat-Neb, as the music at last came to an end. 'You have entertained us well. As a reward, I will take my daughters hunting. We are approaching some fine marshes. There, we shall catch some fat fowl to roast upon the fire tomorrow night.' He beamed at Mut and Isis.

Hopi watched him in disgust. He was behaving as though nothing had happened. He offered no encouragement to the crew, who had done their best to save his life. The man was utterly selfish.

It was a relief that the evening was over. As everyone began to prepare for bed, Tutmose came and sat next to Hopi by the fire.

'Where is the viper?' he whispered.

'It's here,' replied Hopi, indicating his linen bag.

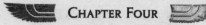

'You won't let it escape, will you?'

Hopi shook his head. 'No.'

'Good.' The doctor smiled. 'Perhaps you could teach me how to handle it. I have often wondered how it is done.'

'Not now, surely!' exclaimed Hopi, looking around anxiously.

Tutmose shook his head. 'No, no, not now.' He lowered his voice. 'But you could show me at dawn, couldn't you? Before we head to the boat?'

'I suppose so.'

The doctor looked satisfied. He rose, and disappeared into his shelter. Hopi gazed into the flames, thinking. He didn't mind showing Tutmose the viper, of course – that was why he had caught it. But the attack had changed things. The crew were very unhappy, and rightly so. How could Hat-Neb and Tutmose carry on like this, as though everything was the same as before?

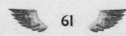

CHAPTER FIVE

Isis awoke with something warm and heavy on her legs. She looked down to see Killer curled up on her covers, fast asleep. She reached to stroke him for a moment, then lay back to think about the night before. She and Mut had seemed to dance for ever. Hat-Neb had demanded more and more; they'd barely had time to catch their breath all evening. But the crew had looked sullen and miserable, and she still had no idea what had really happened to them.

Dawn was filtering through the flaps of the shelter. Isis eased herself from underneath the sleepy cat and crept outside, where some of the crew had begun to stir. Isis wandered towards them. Many seemed tired and grumpy, and Isis could see blood seeping through their bandages. She wished she could talk to them but only Kerem spoke Egyptian, and he was

already busy, marching down to the boat with linen under his arm.

She decided to quiz him anyway. Skipping down the riverbank, she caught up with him and touched his arm. He turned to her in surprise.

'Kerem,' she began, 'is it true that your crew fought off a whole boat of men yesterday, and made them run away?'

Kerem frowned. 'We fought, yes. You can see the injuries.'

'And you fought to protect Hat-Neb, didn't you?' asked Isis. 'It was very loyal and brave of you.'

Kerem gave a short laugh. 'Loyal and brave!' he repeated. He stopped walking and looked at her. 'You understand nothing, little dancer.'

Isis was puzzled. 'Why?'

Kerem shook his head, and carried on walking. 'We fight when we must fight. This is our work. It does not make us loyal or brave. And yesterday we did not fight for long, because your gods came to save us.'

Isis was curious. 'How did the gods save you?' she asked. 'Do you mean Sobek, the crocodile god? Hat-Neb sacrificed two lambs to him before we left.'

Kerem hesitated. 'You ask too many questions,' he said.

'But was it Sobek?' Isis persisted.

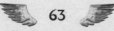

Kerem had reached the boat. He splashed through the shallow water and started hoisting his pile of linen covers up the ladder.

'It was not the crocodile,' he said. 'It was a snake god.'

'A snake god! What snake?' Isis's thoughts immediately flew to Hopi. But what had her brother got to do with it?

'I don't know,' he replied. 'I can't tell you. This is not my land, and these are not my gods.'

And he disappeared over the side of the deck.

The viper's body lay quietly on Hopi's lap. It was fairly small for a horned viper; probably a male, because the females were bigger.

'You see, it's quite docile,' said Hopi. 'If it was a cobra, it would be much more likely to strike.'

It was not long after dawn. Tutmose had shaken him awake, wanting to be taught about viper-handling. Now, as Hopi held it firmly behind the head, he studied the snake intently.

'I see,' he said.

'It's quite calm at the moment,' Hopi explained. 'But if it was cornered in the wild, it might make a warning sound by rubbing its scales together.' He ran a finger down the length of its body. 'They're tough,

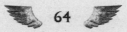

these scales. They make a rasping sound: *fffffff* . . .'

'Fascinating,' said Tutmose.

'Try holding it.' Hopi offered him the viper.

Tentatively, the doctor reached out and stroked the snake's body, then recoiled. 'It's so cold.'

'You haven't touched a snake before? They're always cold.'

Tutmose placed his hand on the viper once more, then pulled a face. He looked nauseous. 'Perhaps this was a bad idea,' he admitted.

Hopi was curious, especially after everything that had happened. 'Why would you need to learn how to handle it anyway?'

Tutmose sighed. 'I'm a doctor,' he said. 'A snake's venom might be useful to me. You can get it, I suppose?'

'Get what? The venom?'

'Yes.'

'Well, I've never milked a viper,' confessed Hopi. 'It's not easy, because you have to make them strike.'

'Could you try? Just to show me?' Tutmose seemed almost excited.

Hopi hesitated, uneasy. 'I could show you in theory,' he said.

'Theory's no good,' said Tutmose impatiently. He stood up, and wandered around the shelter. Then he

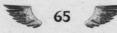

came back to sit close to Hopi. 'Listen,' he said in a low voice, 'you saw what happened yesterday. Our boat came under attack. Hat-Neb is in danger – there are many who would like to see him dead. These men were not the only ones. If he has been attacked once, he will be attacked again.'

'Why?' asked Hopi. 'What has he done?'

The doctor placed a hand on Hopi's shoulder. 'He has a reputation for cruelty,' he said. 'Nevertheless, it is my job to protect him, with magic if necessary. And a snake's venom is full of power. You must know that.'

Hopi said nothing. He didn't want to get involved in Hat-Neb's protection. On the other hand, he didn't want to fall out with Tutmose, either.

'Very well,' he agreed reluctantly. 'I will need a small container – a jar, perhaps – to collect the venom. And a piece of linen,' he said.

Tutmose smiled. 'Good,' he said. 'Today, Hat-Neb is going on a hunting trip in the marshes. We will find a jar on the boat, and you can show me then.'

Isis watched as the crew swung the boat out into the middle of the river. She was thinking. A snake god . . . it was too much of a coincidence. Hopi *must* be involved, and she was determined to work out how.

She found him sitting at the prow of the boat and sat down next to him.

'Hopi,' she said, 'why won't you tell me about yesterday?'

Hopi shifted uncomfortably. 'Tell you what?'

'Kerem told me that they were saved by a snake. A snake god. Do you know anything about that?'

Isis noticed Hopi's hand drifting to his bag. She stared at it. Surely her brother didn't have a snake on board?

'Er, no. No,' said Hopi. 'Nothing to do with me.'

Isis felt stung. She knew her brother too well. 'Don't lie to me, Hopi!' she hissed. 'You have a snake in your basket. I know you do.'

'Isis.' Hopi's voice was urgent. 'Be careful. Keep out of all this. You don't understand.'

'Understand what?' cried Isis. 'What's that horrible doctor done to you, Hopi? You've changed. You've become all dark and sly.'

Hopi looked shocked. 'Don't say that, Isis.' He hesitated. 'Listen. The reason I'm not telling you things is this. You think Hat-Neb and Nebo are kind and strong, and that they'll look after you. But I've told you before: they're not what you think. Last night I saw –'

Isis sprang to her feet. 'You don't know them like I

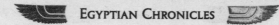
do,' she retorted. 'That doctor has poisoned your mind against them. I'm going to tell Nebo about your snake.'

Hopi grabbed her arm. 'Don't you dare, Isis!'

Isis stared down at him, full of defiance. 'You can't stop me,' she said.

She ran off down the deck to the back of the boat and looked out towards the riverbank, her feelings in turmoil. It was true that Hopi couldn't make her keep quiet, but she had never been disloyal to him before. She hated arguing with him. But she didn't know how to make him see that he was wrong. She folded her arms, wondering what to do. Maybe she wouldn't speak to Nebo *just* yet.

She went into the cabin, where Sheri and Kia were playing their instruments softly. They stopped when Isis came in, and smiled.

'Are you looking forward to your hunting trip, Isis?' asked Sheri. 'You're not afraid of coming across any crocodiles? If you don't want to go, just say so.'

'I think Hat-Neb and Nebo will keep me safe,' replied Isis. She looked at them anxiously. 'They will, won't they?'

'Of course they will,' said Sheri. 'You'll be fine.'

Isis smiled in relief. 'I think it's going to be fun.

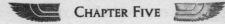

Why don't you want to come?'

Kia laughed. 'We'd rather sit here and relax,' she said. 'You and Mut go and enjoy yourselves.'

They seemed so happy and normal that Isis felt reassured. She kissed them both, then went back outside to find that Kerem had already hired two boats from local fishermen. The little craft were soon loaded up; Isis and Mut clambered in with Hat-Neb, Nebo and Killer the cat, while Kerem followed in the second boat with one of the crew. Isis sat close to Hat-Neb as Nebo began to paddle.

'Are you ready, my daughter?' Hat-Neb asked. 'You will have a wonderful day today, I promise. And I won't let anything harm you. You know that, don't you?'

'Yes.' Isis nodded, and her anger at Hopi welled up once again. Hat-Neb was only ever kind and thoughtful. How could her brother think anything else?

Hopi watched his sister leave in the little boat. There was no doubt about it: Isis had mastered her fear of the river. He was glad for her, of course, but it still hurt, because this man Hat-Neb had driven such a wedge between them. He wondered if she would tell Nebo about the viper. Surely she wouldn't really betray him?

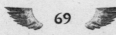

With Kerem gone, the rest of the crew huddled together on the deck, muttering among themselves. Hopi noticed that the two men with the worst injuries were slumped against the rail of the boat. The one that Nebo had punched rocked backwards and forwards, twisting his lip, in a quiet, lost world of pain. For a second, Hopi caught his eye. It shook him. The man's eyes blazed with anger.

Hopi didn't know what to do. He spread his palms, then pointed up at the sky. *'The gods will help you,'* he wanted to say. He must speak to Tutmose – surely he could do more for these men. But the doctor was not on the deck. Hopi glanced at the shore, and to his surprise, there was Tutmose, weaving his way between the vendors on the riverbank.

Where does he think he's going? Hopi thought to himself.

There was only one way to find out. Slinging his bag over his shoulder, Hopi scrambled down the boat's ladder and followed him.

The riverbank was busy, with a bustling market and many people working on papyrus stems – soaking or splitting them, or pressing together the strips to form precious sheets for writing on. The doctor wound through the workers quickly, and Hopi cursed his limp as he left the market and headed along the

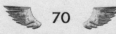

narrow streets. Tutmose stopped to speak to someone, and Hopi slipped into a doorway. He could just hear the doctor's voice.

'My name is Imhotep, from the . . .' He heard Tutmose say. '. . . do you know of . . .'

The rest was lost. Hopi frowned. Imhotep? Why was Tutmose giving another name?

A few more words drifted his way: '. . . of course, yes. I can pay very well.'

Hopi felt reassured. Tutmose must be getting more treatments for the injured men. He peeped around the doorway and saw that the doctor had set off again with a local man by his side. Hopi emerged from the doorway and followed, but people had begun to notice the strangers in their midst. Women stared as he limped along. Then, to his frustration, Tutmose turned down an alleyway and disappeared.

Hopi felt lost. He couldn't just hang around. Reluctantly, he retraced his steps to the boat to wait. There, he found the crew sitting in the shade, their faces sullen. The injured men lay with their eyes closed. Hopi wished that Tutmose would hurry up.

He went into the cabin, where Sheri and Kia were resting. They smiled at him as he came in.

'Is everything all right, Hopi?' asked Sheri.

'I'm not sure,' said Hopi. He hesitated. 'I'm

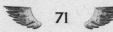

worried about the crew. You know, the ones who were injured.'

Kia frowned. 'Tutmose said that none of them were badly hurt.'

'Yes, but . . . some of them seem quite sick.'

The two women looked at each other. 'I'm sure the doctor knows best, Hopi,' said Sheri quietly.

Hopi fell silent. Sheri and Kia were professionals. Long years of being entertainers at drunken parties had made them cautious, and Hopi knew that they would steer clear of any trouble. So he went back out on to the deck, striding up and down, until at last he saw Tutmose approaching along the riverbank.

'Tutmose!' he exclaimed, as soon as the doctor reached the deck. 'I'm glad you're back. Have you brought more treatments? The crew are growing impatient.'

The doctor barely looked at him. 'They can wait,' he said shortly.

Hopi was taken aback. 'But . . . but they are suffering,' he said. 'And they seem to be getting angry.'

Tutmose shrugged dismissively. 'They are annoyed with Hat-Neb for going hunting,' he said. 'They want to reach their destination. The sooner we get there, the sooner they're paid. Boat crews are all the same.'

He turned his back on Hopi and disappeared into

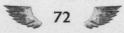

the cabin. Hopi was bewildered. So Tutmose had not been fetching supplies for the crew. He didn't seem to care much about them at all. But if that was the case, what had he been seeking in the town – and why had he used a false name?

Isis closed her eyes as they paddled across the river towards the thick stands of papyrus reeds, with their soft fronds waving in the breeze. As they grew closer, the air filled with the sounds of birds – the twittering of weavers and warblers, the harsher squawks of ducks and geese, and the wild cries of the ibis. Isis opened her eyes again, and was entranced. She forgot that crocodiles might be gliding beneath them. Instead, she felt full of happiness at the beauty of the sunlight glinting through the reeds and sedges.

The Nubian nosed the boat onwards through the thickets, past vibrant blue lotus flowers and mounds of rich silt. Killer stood right at the front, his whole body tense and eager. Hat-Neb stood up and reached for a throwing stick. A duck broke cover, taking to the sky with a loud quack.

Hat-Neb didn't hesitate. He hurled the throwing stick, and it caught the bird neatly across the neck. It fell, fluttering, somewhere ahead, and Killer leaped from the boat. The water was shallow, and the cat

bounded through it, barely wetting his paws. He disappeared between the reeds in the direction of the stricken duck. They waited a few moments, and then Killer returned with the bird dangling from his mouth.

'Good work, Killer!' Hat-Neb praised him.

Killer jumped back into the boat and dropped his catch. He had finished it off with a neat bite to the back of the neck – it was already dead. Isis stroked its warm feathers, feeling a little sorry for it. But she also loved the taste of roasted duck.

It was becoming difficult to take the boat further, because the water was so shallow. Hat-Neb motioned to Nebo to stop paddling. Carefully lifting his linen tunic, he stepped out of the boat.

'We will walk from here,' he said. 'A little river water will not do us any harm. Come, and I will show you how to use a throwing stick.'

Isis took his hand and stepped out, followed by Mut. This was a strange, wonderful world: stands of papyrus reeds towered high above her head, and the lotus flowers were dazzling. She picked a delicate blue bloom, and tucked it into her hair as Hat-Neb waded slowly forward.

Another duck – and he threw his second stick. Again, the bird fell, squawking, and Killer leaped to fetch it.

Hat-Neb handed Isis a stick. It was gently curved

with a kink at one end, and he showed her how to hold it.

'If you miss, don't worry,' he told her. 'I have plenty more and we can collect them all later.'

Isis held the smooth, strong wood. She was sure she would never be able to throw it hard enough. 'Like this?' she asked.

But Hat-Neb didn't reply. She turned to look at him. Beads of sweat stood on his forehead, and his hand was clutched to his neck. With a choking sound, he sank to his knees in the mud. Then, slowly, he toppled over.

CHAPTER SIX

Isis screamed, and dropped to her knees by Hat-Neb's head. He was covered in mud and quite unconscious. She and Mut tried to lift him, but he was much too heavy.

Nebo appeared through the reeds. 'You let me,' he said. 'I do it.'

The two girls moved to one side to let him take their place. Even for the strong guard, Hat-Neb was a lot to manage. The Nubian grunted as he shifted his master into a sitting position in the mud.

'Is he still breathing?' asked Mut anxiously.

Nebo said nothing. His face was grim as the other boat crew appeared. 'You help me,' the Nubian growled, looking at Kerem. 'We put him in the boat.'

Kerem and the other man stepped forward, and each grasped one of Hat-Neb's thighs. With Nebo lift-

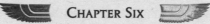

ing his shoulders, they managed to carry him back to the boat and flop him into it. Hat-Neb stirred. His eyes flickered. He groaned, and his muscles twitched. Then, all at once, he came to life and vomited violently over the side of the boat. Isis clutched Mut's arm. This was all so frightening and horrible. No one seemed to know what to do; even Nebo seemed unsure.

Blindly, Hat-Neb wiped a hand over his face. He opened his eyes and stared around, his eyes glassy.

'Drink some water,' said Nebo, reaching for a flagon in the bottom of the boat. He lifted it to Hat-Neb's mouth, making him take several large gulps. More dribbled down his chin and on to his linen tunic.

'Enough,' gasped Hat-Neb, spluttering.

Killer appeared with the second duck in his mouth, which he dropped silently near the boat. Then he leaped inside and miaowed, his tail twitching. Hat-Neb moved his hand vaguely, and placed it on the cat's head.

'Killer,' he mumbled. 'Good cat.' He coughed, then struggled to push himself upright. He looked around, his eyes growing clearer now, and registered the circle of faces staring at him anxiously. 'Well,' he said. 'What's happened here then?'

'We go back to the boat,' said Nebo. 'You are sick.'

'Nonsense,' said Hat-Neb weakly. 'I am Hat-Neb. The gods protect me. I am fine.'

The Nubian nodded his head at Kerem, asking him to push the little boat back into deeper water. Together, the three men eased it out of the shallows.

'You get in,' the Nubian told Isis. 'Come, I help you.'

Still feeling a little afraid, Isis took his arm and clambered back into the boat.

'Don't look so upset, little Isis,' said Hat-Neb. 'Just the effects of fine wine.'

But Isis saw that he was gripping the sides of the boat, and a pale, greenish sheen seemed to shine through the deep gold of his skin.

Hopi couldn't bear to stay on the deck any longer. The eyes of the crew followed him everywhere. But he didn't want to go into the cabin, either, where Tutmose must be sitting enjoying himself with Sheri and Kia. Perhaps they were right. Perhaps it was just a case of waiting until they reached their destination. But the atmosphere on the deck was getting steadily worse, and Hopi longed to escape.

He reached the hatch that led from the deck into the cramped hold and peered into it. Awkwardly, he

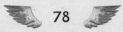

clambered down the steep, narrow steps, allowing his eyes to adjust to the darkness. At first, he thought there was nothing there – nothing but foul-smelling water swilling around the bottom. But then he began to see more in the gloom: on wooden boards above the water sat sacks of grain, flagons of beer and wine, and caskets of other foodstuffs. Of course – this was where Hat-Neb kept his supplies. There were finer goods, too – bowls, caskets and statues of wood and stone, some of them representing Hat-Neb himself. Hopi listened to the Nile waters lapping the hull of the boat, and gave a sigh of relief. It was much more peaceful than on deck.

A scuttling, squeaking sound caught his attention. There were rats down here! He felt a thrill of excitement. His viper could catch one – it would be wonderful to watch it hunt. He reached for his papyrus basket, then hesitated. Was it really wise to let the viper loose? He weighed it up in his mind. Hat-Neb and the others wouldn't be back for hours – they had taken their lunch with them. The crew had nothing to do, and no reason to visit the hold. There would be plenty of time to catch the snake before the others returned.

His mind made up, he pulled the papyrus basket from his bag. He wedged it between two sacks, took

off the lid and watched as the viper slowly emerged, on full alert, to explore its new environment. At once the snake headed into the darkness between the bags of grain. Hopi felt a pang of anxiety. He couldn't see it now. Perhaps this wasn't such a good idea after all . . .

'Hopi!' A voice made him jump. It was Tutmose.

Hopi squinted up at the hatch. 'I'm here.'

The doctor's face peered down at him. 'What are you doing in there? Come on up.'

Hopi looked around the hold. The snake had completely disappeared. 'Yes, coming,' he called, trying to catch a glimpse of the viper.

'Well, come on then,' insisted Tutmose.

There was no choice. He'd just have to find the snake later. Reluctantly, Hopi climbed back up the ladder and out into the bright daylight.

The doctor seemed surprisingly cheerful. 'So,' he said, 'you were going to teach me something. You haven't forgotten, I hope?' He held out a small ceramic jar from the cabin, along with a piece of linen.

'Oh!' Hopi was startled. Panic rose in his chest. He had hoped that Tutmose had forgotten the idea – and now the snake was no longer in his basket. 'N-no . . . it's just that . . .'

'Come, we will go to the far shelter.' Tutmose

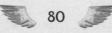

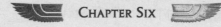

smiled. 'No one will disturb us there.'

Hopi tried to smile back, but couldn't. He gazed down the deck and saw that the crew were watching them, their eyes flitting from Hopi to the doctor and back again. He took a deep breath.

'I . . . I can't,' he said. 'I'm sorry, Tutmose. I don't think the viper can be milked after all – it's not like a cobra. I think it's better left alone.'

'What's changed your mind?' Tutmose seemed annoyed.

Hopi didn't know what to say. He couldn't think of an excuse.

Tutmose looked at him closely. 'You've released it, haven't you?' he demanded.

'No, no – well, not exactly,' stuttered Hopi.

'Show me your basket.'

It was no use. He would have to tell Tutmose what he had done. 'It's down there. In the hold,' Hopi whispered.

'What? Loose?' Tutmose almost shouted.

'Sshhh. It's perfectly safe. I've let it out so that it can catch a rat, if it wants to. I'll catch it again before anyone needs to go down there.'

The doctor's face filled with anger. 'How could you be so stupid?' he hissed.

Hopi scrambled towards the hatch. 'I'll catch it

again right away,' he said hurriedly. 'I was going to anyway. I'm sorry, Tutmose.'

But at that moment there were shouts further along the deck. The crew were on their feet, calling and pointing. Hopi and Tutmose looked out across the Nile to see what the fuss was about. There, just a few paddles' length away, was the hunting expedition that had set off only a few hours before.

Isis started calling. 'Hopi! Sheri! Kia!' she cried, waving her arms as the little fishing boats reached the shore.

The fishing boats' owners appeared, looking very surprised to see their property back so soon. Hat-Neb stepped out, swaying, and cursing under his breath. Nebo steadied him, and he tottered up the bank.

'I must complain to my wine merchant,' he muttered. With great determination, he struggled across the little harbour to clamber up the ladder of his own boat, then stood leaning on the rail to catch his breath.

Isis followed him up. The first person she saw was Hopi, who was staring at them as though they had come back from the Next World, not just the west bank marshes.

Hat-Neb gulped a few deep breaths, then turned to Kerem. 'Tell your men to bring up all the flagons of wine from the hold,' he ordered. 'I want to inspect

them. Then set sail for Djeba.' Still staggering, he walked along the deck and disappeared into the cabin.

Isis saw the alarm on Hopi's face as the crew gathered around Kerem. The captain began to give orders and her brother suddenly interrupted.

'Kerem, let me fetch the flagons,' he said. 'It will help your men. I have nothing else to do.'

Fetch the flagons? Isis stared at her brother. Whatever was he thinking of, taking on the work of the crew? He'd never manage it, not with his injured leg.

'You can't!' she exclaimed. 'They're heavy, Hopi. It's not your job.'

'Shut up, Isis.' Hopi looked furious. 'Just keep out of it. I've told you before.'

'But you *can't*!' Isis felt tears of indignation surfacing. It had been such an awful morning, and now this! Hopi was being really stupid. 'They *are* heavy. Why can't the crew do it?'

Hopi stared at her. A flicker of despair crossed his face, and all of a sudden she realised that this had nothing to do with the flagons of wine. He wanted to go into the hold for some other reason. An important reason. But now it was too late.

'Isis asks a very good question.' It was Nebo who spoke. He must have been watching ever since they'd

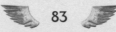

come back on board. 'Why you want to do this, Hopi?'

Hopi's shoulders sagged. 'I just wanted to help,' he said weakly. Then, with a spark of anger, he glared at Nebo. 'Some of the crew are injured, if you hadn't noticed.'

Nebo nodded. 'Ah, the crew, the crew,' he said, in a mocking tone. He stepped towards the hatch, and gestured down at it with an open hand. 'Come then, Hopi. Now you care for the crew so much, we go into the hold. You and me, we go together. This is very good idea, yes?'

And Isis knew, with a sinking heart, that she had somehow dumped her brother right in it.

Hopi descended the steps slowly, thinking fast. There would be no hope of catching the viper now. He would have to make a show of moving the flagons, and hope for the best. Nebo was much too tall for the little hold and stayed at the bottom of the ladder as Hopi put down his bag. There was no sign of the snake. Hopi reached for the first of the wine flagons and picked it up. Isis was right. It was very heavy. There was no way he could carry it up the narrow steps on his own.

But he would have to try. With a grunt, he picked

up the flagon and staggered over the wobbly boards towards Nebo. He deposited it at the fan-bearer's feet, then went and picked up another.

'Stop this. You are being very stupid.' Nebo's deep voice was angry.

Hopi ignored him. He dropped the second flagon next to the first, and reached for a third. He shifted it, easing his hands underneath it, then stopped and stared. The viper was there, hiding behind the flagon. It moved slowly, sluggishly, and Hopi immediately saw why. Just behind its head, the viper's body had swollen into a big lump. It had caught and swallowed a rat.

There was a movement at his shoulder, and he realised that the fan-bearer had stooped down to creep up behind him. Nebo had seen the snake. His breathing was fast and shallow, and Hopi realised that he was afraid.

'You bring big problem on this boat,' said the fan-bearer.

Hopi felt a surge of anger. He shook his head. 'No,' he said. 'You don't understand. It was this snake that saved us.'

But Nebo wasn't listening. 'A snake is danger,' he insisted. 'A snake brings sickness.'

'This snake hasn't harmed anyone!' cried Hopi.

'I've kept it safe the whole time – it's been in my papyrus basket. I only just let it loo—'

'Now I see why you keep this basket and stick.' Nebo's voice was low with menace. 'You tell me big lies. I do not like lies. You catch it.' The guard's fingers dug into Hopi's shoulder. 'You catch it and you bring to show Hat-Neb.' He stepped back to the ladder, and waited.

Hopi knew when he was defeated. He picked up his stick and bag, and approached the snake. Sensing his presence, it shifted its coils and rasped at him. *Ffffff*. But, weighed down with its meal, it had no desire to move quickly. With a flick of his stick, Hopi captured it, lowered it into the basket and replaced the lid.

The Nubian nodded grimly, and turned towards the steps. 'Follow me,' he instructed Hopi, and began to climb towards the daylight.

Isis watched anxiously as Nebo reappeared out of the hold with Hopi behind him. Nebo gave Hopi a push towards the cabin. Isis followed them in. Hat-Neb was lying down, his eyes closed, while Sheri wiped his forehead with a damp piece of linen.

'Master,' said Nebo, 'this boy, he is nothing but trouble.'

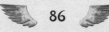

Sheri and Kia looked up in alarm. 'Hopi!' exclaimed Sheri. 'What have you done?'

'N-nothing,' said Hopi. 'I caught a viper, that's all.'

'Show it,' ordered Nebo.

Hopi lifted his linen bag from his shoulder. Isis saw him throw a warning glance at Mut, knowing she was terrified of snakes, then reached for his basket. Mut dropped Killer and ran out of the cabin, while Hat-Neb's eyes bulged with curiosity. Isis craned her neck to see the viper, which lay lazily in Hopi's hands.

'It's just eaten a rat, sir,' he said, as though that could explain everything.

Sheri and Kia looked horrified. 'Oh, Hopi.' Kia's voice was reproachful. 'What were you thinking of?'

'You don't even know what happened,' retorted Hopi. 'This viper broke up the fight between the boat crews. It has done only good, and no harm.'

Hat-Neb grunted. 'A likely story.'

'It's true.'

Hopi's eyes were bright with defiance, and in spite of everything, Isis felt a rush of loyalty towards her brother. She swallowed hard. 'I know it's true,' she piped up. 'Kerem told me. He said a snake god had saved them.'

'*Saved* them?' Kia sounded incredulous.

'The barge crew were afraid of it. That's why they

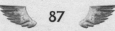

stopped fighting,' said Hopi.

Silence fell. Hat-Neb seemed to be thinking.

It was Kia who spoke. 'But even if this is true, Hopi, why did you bring it on board?'

'I didn't think it was a good idea,' said Hopi. 'But Tutmose told me I should.'

'Did he indeed?' Hat-Neb stroked his chin. 'Where is he? Bring him here.'

Kia went out on to the deck to find the doctor. In the meantime, the cabin fell silent once more. Isis felt her palms sweating. Hat-Neb and Nebo were both looking very serious.

Tutmose walked in. 'What is it, sir?' he asked.

Hat-Neb waved his hand in Hopi's direction. 'I believe you are responsible for this.'

The doctor appeared startled to see the viper. 'A snake! Whatever do you mean?'

Hopi looked dismayed. 'You told me to bring it on board!' he exclaimed.

Tutmose gave a cracked laugh. 'Absurd,' he said. 'I've never seen this creature before in my life.' He made a show of looking closely at the snake from different angles, then turned back to Hat-Neb. 'But I can tell you what it is. This is a horned viper. You will be pleased to hear that it is not as dangerous as a cobra, but it is a menace, all the same. Most irresponsible to

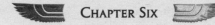
bring such a thing on to the boat.'

Hat-Neb leaned back on his cushions and turned to the other adults in the room. 'I have no choice,' he said, his voice regretful. 'Tutmose is right: this is a danger, a danger to us all. The boy must be punished.' He sighed, as though it were a great inconvenience.

Isis felt herself go cold. She knew that Hopi had told the truth. Everyone waited, tense.

Hat-Neb reflected for a moment. Then he gave a shrug. 'Shut him in the hold,' he instructed. 'See if he enjoys having nothing but a snake for company.'

Hopi's face was still as he lowered the viper back into its basket. He didn't look at anyone as he followed Nebo out of the cabin. All Isis could think of, as she watched the hatch being closed over him, was how it would feel to be alone, shut in the hold in the darkness.

CHAPTER SEVEN

Hopi heard the hatch bang shut. He groped his way over to the stores of grain and flung himself down on the sacks. He was furious. Tutmose had betrayed him! After all that talk about the snake . . . Hopi couldn't believe it. He thumped the sack of grain beneath him, reliving the look in the doctor's eyes as he had lied outright. How could he! How *could* he?

Eventually he calmed down. It was very dark, but slowly his eyes adjusted. He could hear the footsteps on the deck above, the lapping of the Nile waters and the creaking of the wooden planks. And he could hear voices, but they were too muffled to understand. He soon found that he didn't mind his punishment too much. It was actually quite peaceful. The warm air in the hold made him drowsy, and he drifted off to sleep.

When he woke, he was hungry. He could just about

see, so he could tell that night had not yet fallen. He clambered over to the food caskets, opened one and felt inside. Dried figs! He stuffed one into his mouth before moving on to the next casket. That one was full of dates, and the next one packed with raisins. Hopi grinned. He wasn't going to be hungry for long.

His stomach full, he began to feel bored. He decided to explore the hold more thoroughly, for something to do. He felt his way along the food stores – sacks of emmer wheat and barley, dried lentils and beans, a sealed pot of honey, rich pastries. There were all the mats, stakes and linens for the camp shelters. Then came a row of statues, carved in both wood and stone . . . and at the end of the hold, animal skins, cured and made into hangings and rugs.

The light was fading. His exploration complete, Hopi groped his way back along the sides of the hold, feeling the lining of thick grass that was supposed to soak up any leaks in the wooden planking. And then he stopped. His fingers touched something different. A leather pouch, buried in a thick tuft of grass. Hopi pulled it out. The pouch had a leather thong that tied it shut at the top. Fumbling in excitement, he undid the knot.

Inside, there were two little bottles, three smaller pouches and a tiny box. Hopi brought them out, one

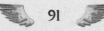

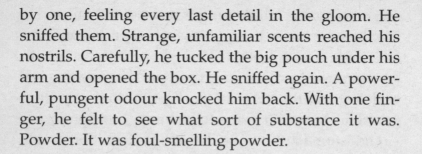

by one, feeling every last detail in the gloom. He sniffed them. Strange, unfamiliar scents reached his nostrils. Carefully, he tucked the big pouch under his arm and opened the box. He sniffed again. A powerful, pungent odour knocked him back. With one finger, he felt to see what sort of substance it was. Powder. It was foul-smelling powder.

The women and girls watched as Tutmose examined Hat-Neb, peering down his throat and pulling back his eyelids.

'You will be perfectly well tomorrow,' he said. 'You are right. There must be something wrong with your wine.'

'Thought so.' Hat-Neb gave a satisfied grunt. 'Well, I know how to deal with bad wine merchants. He'll regret it. Now I'm going to sleep.'

The fat overseer rested his head on a pile of cushions and soon began to snore loudly. He didn't seem the slightest bit sorry about Hopi. Isis felt distraught.

'Don't worry,' whispered Sheri. 'Hopi will be fine. We're arriving tomorrow. It's not for long.'

'But Tutmose *lied*,' Isis whispered back. 'I know he did.'

Sheri squeezed her hand. 'Isis, Hopi shouldn't

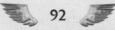

have brought a snake on to the boat. Whatever the doctor may have done, Hopi had to be punished. It will do him no harm.'

Isis didn't think so. Hopi had nothing but rats and a viper for company. And if he said he hadn't wanted to bring the snake on board, then he hadn't. She got up and went out on to the deck. Perhaps she would be able to communicate with him somehow. But when she stepped outside, she saw at once that there were other problems on board. Kerem and Nebo were in the middle of a big argument.

'Half the crew not working,' Nebo was saying. 'We do not pay lazy men.'

Kerem shook his head furiously. 'We fight for you. We injured for you. Two men are very sick.'

Nebo towered over the captain. His face was ugly and menacing, and Isis was shocked. She had never seen him look like that before.

'You do what I tell you,' he growled.

But Kerem wasn't intimidated. He folded his arms. 'We are many,' he said. 'And you are few.'

Nebo drew himself up very tall. His eyes flashed, and he flexed his huge muscles. 'I can *snap* you,' he said. 'You will see.'

He turned away, and for the first time, he saw Isis watching him. But his expression didn't change. His

eyes were cold. Isis felt as though he looked straight through her. Then he marched past her and into the cabin.

Hopi put everything back into the pouch. Menna had taught him about many powders and potions, which he combined with magic to treat scorpion stings and snake bites, but he didn't recognise any of the smells and textures he'd found here. He knew there was only one man on the boat who was likely to have a secret supply of such things, and that was Tutmose.

Why had Tutmose hidden these supplies in the depths of the hold? He kept most of his medicines in the cabin, where they were easily reached. Hopi lay back on the sacks, thinking. Perhaps, after all, Isis was right – perhaps the doctor *was* up to something. Hopi remembered her story about Hat-Neb's fan. It was a magical, powerful object, and deep down, Hopi knew that Tutmose had no business touching it . . . unless it was to tamper with its magic in some way.

And then there was his mysterious visit to the town that morning. A doctor could have found normal medical supplies easily enough, if he'd wanted to. He didn't have to sneak around using a false name. Hopi's hand drifted to the viper's basket. Tutmose had taken an interest in Hopi's skills from

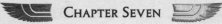

the word go. And he had felt so flattered by it! He had thought that the doctor held him in genuine respect. Hopi's heart clouded with anger once more as he thought of how Tutmose had betrayed him. Now he could see that the doctor had his own agenda. And slowly Hopi was realising what it might be . . .

It was now very dark in the hold, and Hopi listened for signs that they were heading to shore. Someone would have to come down to the cabin for supplies before nightfall. Sure enough, there was a scraping of wood as the hatch opened, and feet climbed down the ladder. It was Kerem and two of the crew.

Kerem bowed to Hopi respectfully. 'We need to take food and shelter to the deck,' he said.

'Of course,' said Hopi. 'Go ahead.'

The crew members began to hoist the linen camp shelters on to their backs, while Kerem stared at Hopi curiously. 'This is strange place to sit. What are you doing down here?'

'Don't you know?' Hopi shrugged. 'Hat-Neb and Nebo are punishing me.'

'Punishing you!' Kerem looked shocked. 'But you the priest. You still have the snake god?'

'Yes, he's still here,' replied Hopi. 'He's safe.' He indicated his bag.

'Why do they punish you?'

Hopi gave a wry smile. 'They don't respect the snake god,' he said. 'They don't want it on board.'

Kerem's face darkened. 'These men –' he said. 'We have had enough.' He glanced back at the hatch to check that no one else was there. 'They think we are stupid and desperate. They treat us very bad. Maybe you do not see this, but it is true.'

Hopi thought of the injured man crumpling to the ground as Nebo punched him. 'I have seen it. I know how Nebo behaves. He and Hat-Neb are both evil.'

'Yes. It is more than our honour will bear. We will not take it any more. And there is something else.' Kerem's eyes flashed. 'We have no reason to serve him longer, because of what we heard on the river-bank. You remember the men that we fight? They laugh at us. They say we will never be paid in Djeba. And now we think they are right.'

Hopi did remember. He pictured the leader heading back to the tug, calling over his shoulder, *'If that motley crew of yours think they'll get a fortune in Djeba, they are even more foolish than they look . . .'*

'Whatever we do, we do it before we get to Djeba,' Kerem carried on. 'When we get to the town, it will be too late. There will be many others to protect him.'

His men were now loaded up with mats, rugs and stakes for building shelters. He nodded to them, and they began to climb to the deck. Then he turned back to Hopi. 'You saved us once,' he said. 'Are you with us now?'

Hopi hesitated. He wasn't sure what Kerem had planned, or if there was anything that he could do to help. But if the captain wanted support against Hat-Neb and Nebo, he should surely give it.

'Yes,' he said. 'I'm with you.'

Kerem nodded, satisfied. 'Good.' He picked up a casket of figs, and headed out of the hold.

Isis was still on the deck. She had tried peering through the planks into the hold, but she couldn't see a thing. When Kerem emerged, she ran to him.

'Kerem,' she asked, 'is Hopi all right?'

The captain looked at her. 'He is well enough. But this punishment is a great evil,' he muttered darkly. 'Hat-Neb thinks he is strong, but no one can fight the gods.'

His words frightened Isis. It was getting dark, and the men were not behaving as they usually did at this hour. They moved slowly, sullenly, and some were doing nothing at all.

Nebo appeared out of the cabin. 'What is happen-

ing?' demanded the fan-bearer. 'Darkness is coming. Why are we not going to shore?'

The crew members looked at each other. They might not speak Egyptian, but they understood Nebo clearly enough. Before Kerem could answer, one of them stepped forward and made a rude gesture, right in the fan-bearer's face.

Nebo's response was like lightning. He grabbed the man's arm and spun him around so that his arm was twisted at a terrible angle up his back. Then, with his other hand, Nebo wrenched the man's elbow. There was a ghastly crunching, tearing sound. The man screamed. Nebo threw him down on the deck and watched him howl in agony.

'I told you,' he said, looking around at the men. 'If you do not do what I say, there is easy answer for me.'

Isis stared at Nebo in disbelief. This was the man who had promised to protect her, but he had just done . . . *that*. It was terrible. She couldn't move. Her throat felt dry. And now things were happening fast. The crew were gathering together, shoulder to shoulder. Silently, they drew weapons. Kerem spoke to one of them, and he disappeared into the hold. When he came back, he brought with him Hopi, carrying his basket in his arms.

Night had fallen. The moon had not yet risen, and

the boat was drifting on the Nile. One of the men held a flaming torch in his hand, which cast eerie shadows across the deck.

'You will not break us.' Kerem faced the fan-bearer with a curved bronze dagger in his hand. 'We suffer, yes. But we are strong, and the snake god is with us.'

Nebo sneered, but Isis saw that he was afraid. 'The boy is nothing,' he retorted. 'And you are nothing. You mercenaries all the same. All you think of is gold. But if you touch me, there will be no gold.'

Kerem's eyes filled with hatred. 'This what you think,' he said. 'But you know nothing about us. The sick men my brothers.' Then he pointed to the man that Nebo had injured. 'This man my uncle's son.' He lifted the tip of his dagger so that it just touched the fan-bearer's throat. 'Some things more important than gold.'

CHAPTER EIGHT

Hopi stood alongside Kerem in the flickering torch-light. He saw his sister's terrified face. He saw the sweat and agony of the injured man lying slumped on one side of the deck. He saw the smouldering anger in Nebo's eyes, and the fear mixed with fury in the eyes of the crew. He reached for his basket. The men feared the viper, but it would give them strength to know it was on their side.

He lifted it out, and raised it above his head.

The men cowered, but Kerem spoke sharply. 'The priest is with us!' he said in Egyptian, then switched to their own language, his voice full of fire and passion. The men listened, and they stood up straighter, inspired by their leader's words.

But now Nebo was no longer alone. Tutmose appeared out of the cabin, and by his side was Hat-Neb.

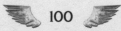

The overseer glared at the crew. 'What do you want from me?' he growled.

Kerem still had his sword pointed in Nebo's direction. 'What we wanted you did not give,' he said. 'We have our honour. We wanted respect; we have received nothing but more injuries. And so now, it is too late. There is only one thing we want.'

Hat-Neb sneered. 'And what is that?'

Kerem nodded to his men. They all raised their weapons. 'We want your life,' he said.

A tense silence fell. Almost imperceptibly, Kerem's men were closing in on Hat-Neb. But Hat-Neb did not look afraid. Instead, he whispered something into Nebo's ear, and the fan-bearer gave a slight nod. Isis was still watching from around the side of the cabin. Hat-Neb turned to her.

'My daughter,' he said, in a husky voice, 'come. This is not a scene for your eyes. Come into the cabin, where it is safe.'

Hopi watched as his sister stepped nervously past the crew. Too late, a warning rose in his throat. Isis was almost at the entrance to the cabin. As she brushed past Nebo, the fan-bearer grabbed her, and slung her under his massive arm.

'No!' shouted Hopi.

Isis yelped, and thrashed out in shock. But the fan-

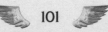

bearer held her fast. One arm pinned her shoulders, while the other reached into his kilt. Hopi almost buckled in horror. In one swift movement, Nebo had drawn a dagger, and had put it to Isis's neck.

Isis's heart was beating so loudly that she could scarcely hear. She tried to wriggle, but Nebo was ten times too strong for her. All she could move were her eyes, which she swivelled around to the faces in front of her. Hopi looked sick with fear.

'Do you know who this is?' Hat-Neb's voice was relaxed and smooth as he waved his hand towards Isis.

'Let her go!' shouted Hopi.

But no one else spoke. Hat-Neb smiled. 'This is the sister of your precious snake priest,' he said to Kerem. 'If you make a single move against us, Nebo will cut her throat. Do you think your priest will support you then?'

Isis felt so thin and fragile pinned to Nebo's side. She wanted to cry, but she was too frightened. She implored Hopi with her eyes, but she could see he was helpless, too. Hat-Neb was horribly clever.

Kerem spat on the deck. 'You think you have won,' he said, lowering his dagger.

'I generally do,' said Hat-Neb. 'Now, enough of this nonsense. Tonight we shall not go ashore. Your men will anchor the boat here and we shall make

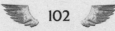

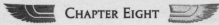

ourselves comfortable the best we can. And then, in the morning, you will guide the boat into Djeba, where everyone will disembark. Is that clear?'

'The gods bring justice,' was Kerem's reply. 'You think you can do anything. But nothing good comes to a man like you.'

The crew slowly backed off, but Nebo was taking no chances. If anything, his grip on Isis tightened. As Hat-Neb followed Tutmose back into the cabin, he carried her in after them, the dagger still dangerously close to her throat.

'Isis!' gasped Sheri. She stared at Nebo. 'What are you doing with her? Let her go!'

'Now, come, don't make a fuss,' said Hat-Neb. 'We have a little problem with this rabble of a crew. She makes a good guarantee, that's all.'

'A guarantee!' Sheri was aghast. 'How dare you! Let her go at once, and take us to shore!'

But Nebo did nothing of the sort. He positioned Isis in a corner of the cabin, where she was trapped. 'You can sleep here,' he told her, then leaned closer. 'And don't try to escape. There is nowhere to go. This . . .' He flicked his dagger, so that the blade glinted. '. . . this the only friend you will find.'

Hopi lowered the viper back into its basket. He felt numb. He had known that Hat-Neb was cruel, but he had not imagined that anyone could be quite this cruel. As the crew milled around the deck, talking among themselves, he gazed over to the dark fields, and a wave of hopelessness washed over him.

'Come, Hopi.' Kerem was at his elbow. 'Come and sit with me.'

The captain guided him to the shelter at the prow of the boat, where the injured men were lying. One of the crew brought a little oil lamp, and they sat down on the bare planks.

'Kerem,' said Hopi in a low voice, 'do you think my sister will be safe?'

Kerem stroked his grey beard. 'I do not know. These men . . . they might do anything. They could kill her, if we betray you.'

Hopi's heart beat faster. He swallowed. 'And . . . and are you going to betray me?'

Kerem said nothing for a moment. He looked at the injured men, their foreheads shining with sweat. He looked at his gnarled knuckles. Then he turned to Hopi and fixed him with his dark eyes. 'We are tough men,' he said. 'We sail. We fight. We know we may die. But we are not animals.' He shook his head. 'We would never kill a little girl. There is justice in this

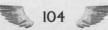

world, and we have our own gods to fear. Not just the snake god.'

Hopi breathed a sigh of relief. So Isis was safe – from Kerem at least.

But Kerem's next words were not so reassuring.

'We will find a way to kill him,' said the captain. 'This man and his guard. You see. We will find a way. Before the morning they both dead.' He made a gesture with his finger across his throat.

'No. No. You can't.' Hopi shook his head. He felt desperate. 'That's the whole point. They will kill Isis before you kill them. And they will kill many of you, too. Please, please . . .'

Kerem's eyes glittered. He laid a hand on Hopi's shoulder. 'There is always a way.'

'But not *this* way!' Hopi was dismayed.

The captain gave a cynical smile.

Hopi was silent, but he was thinking furiously. There had to be a way out of this . . . He got up slowly, and wandered out along the deck, into the darkness. He gazed up at the stars, thinking over everything he knew. Time was running out. Even now, Kerem had called his crew to start plotting . . . plotting to take Nebo by surprise. But the Nubian was so strong and vigilant; Isis was surely doomed.

A shooting star blazed across the sky, falling to

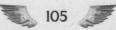

nothingness near the horizon. And suddenly, Hopi saw a chink of light. Of course: the pouch of potions . . . He hurried back to the prow, where Kerem sat crouched with his men.

'What did Hat-Neb say he would pay you?'

Kerem looked up. 'What?'

'He promised you a big payment,' said Hopi, 'didn't he?'

The captain frowned. 'He promised each of us gold, to the value of twenty *debens* of copper,' he said eventually.

It was a huge sum for a few days' work. Hopi almost gasped. 'I see,' he managed to say.

'Why do you ask?' Kerem looked curious.

Hopi controlled himself. He took a deep breath. 'I can get you this gold,' he said calmly.

Kerem laughed. '*You!*'

'You think that you want revenge,' said Hopi. He crouched down with the men, and looked around at their rugged faces. 'But gold is much more useful.'

The captain shrugged. 'Yes, but you think we get the gold now?' Kerem shook his head. 'Hat-Neb would kill a little girl. Whatever you think you can say to him, we will never see this gold.'

Hopi leaned closer. 'There is something you do not know.'

'And what is that?'

'I can't tell you yet.' Hopi's heart was beating fast. 'It is knowledge that only I can use. It has been given to me by the gods. But I promise you, on my own life, that if you deliver us all to Djeba safely, you will receive your gold.'

The captain clearly thought Hopi was mad. 'You are trying to protect your sister.'

'Of course.' Hopi couldn't deny it. 'But think. If you try to kill Hat-Neb, you will lose many things. You will lose your gold. If Isis is killed, you will lose the goodwill of the gods. You may also lose your free-dom – and even your life.'

'True,' said Kerem. 'But if we do as you say, we shall lose both the gold and our honour.'

'No,' said Hopi. 'I have already told you. I promise this gold with my life. And your honour . . .' He paused, searching for the right words. 'If it depends upon a man like Hat-Neb, then honour does not count for very much.'

'Brave words!' exclaimed Kerem.

'Trust me,' said Hopi fervently. 'You will see.'

Isis couldn't sleep. Hat-Neb's snores filled the cabin, while Nebo sat still and silent beside her. She heard drifting murmurs from the crew, talking in low voices

to each other on the deck. The darkness was fearful, but Isis dreaded the dawn. What would happen then? Would there be a battle? Would she survive if there was?

Halfway through the night, Hat-Neb's snores suddenly stopped. Isis listened. He seemed to have stopped breathing altogether. Then, with a choking sound, he woke and jerked himself upright. Isis watched in the gloom. Hat-Neb coughed and retched. Everyone was sitting up now. Tutmose lit an oil lamp, and crept to the overseer's side.

'Drink this,' he said, handing Hat-Neb a beaker.

Hat-Neb took it, and glugged the liquid noisily. 'Urgh,' he moaned when it was finished, clutching his stomach.

'You will sleep again now,' said the doctor.

Isis thought of their trip to the marshes that morning, and the way Hat-Neb had collapsed. How differently she felt now. After all that had happened, she almost wished Hat-Neb were dead. She looked over at Sheri and Kia. Mut was tucked securely between them and Isis envied her.

'Are you all right?' Sheri mouthed at her.

Isis nodded dumbly. She lay back down again, staring at the roof of the cabin.

Tutmose put out the lamp, but the atmosphere in

the cabin remained thick and heavy. Isis was sure that no one else was asleep, or even sleepy. There were just six tense people, and one sick one. Killer padded through the cabin with a soft yowl, but everyone ignored him.

Dawn broke at last. The crew were huddled, dozing, on the deck. There had been no more plotting, and no attack. Now they woke and stretched. Kerem placed two guards by the cabin door, and ordered the others to set sail. Hopi breathed a sigh of relief. It looked as though they would carry on to Djeba after all.

The first person to appear from the cabin was Tutmose. He looked haggard, his thin face even more drawn than usual.

'I need to go down to the hold,' he said, pointing to the hatch.

Kerem wasn't taking any chances. He called another crew member to accompany the doctor. Hopi watched them disappear, and felt his heart beat a little faster. He could guess exactly what the doctor was after.

Tutmose re-emerged a few minutes later, his eyes wild. He looked around the members of the crew, then fixed his gaze on Hopi. Hopi leaned on the rail of the boat, determined to look casual.

'Hopi!' The doctor's voice was desperate. 'I've lost something. Something important. You haven't . . . ?' He trailed off.

'What sort of thing?' Hopi kept his voice very innocent.

The doctor stamped his foot in frustration. 'You were down there! You –' Again he broke off. 'You must help me,' he finished, lowering his voice.

Hopi stared at him coldly, remembering how the doctor had betrayed him. 'I don't even know what you're talking about.'

Tutmose stared hard at Hopi's bag. 'The thing I'm looking for . . . it could help you. It could help all of us. Even the crew. Tell the crew. Let them know that I can solve everything.'

'I've told you,' said Hopi. 'If you've lost something, it has nothing to do with me.'

CHAPTER NINE

'We approach Djeba,' announced Nebo, standing at the entrance to the cabin.

Hat-Neb sat up. He looked tired and ill, with big circles under his eyes. He looked blearily around the cabin. 'We are all alive, I see,' he commented.

'The danger has passed. The crew can do nothing. Too many people here.'

Isis could hear them – children's voices calling from the riverbank, men shouting, someone's donkey braying. She realised she had survived, and felt weak with relief.

Hat-Neb staggered to his feet, donned a clean linen kilt and went out on to the deck.

Nebo nodded to Isis, Mut and the women. 'You may come,' he said.

The riverbank swarmed with people. Children

 111

pointed at the beautiful vessel, shouting, and a flotilla of little fishing boats bobbed on the water around them. Hat-Neb went to the rail of the boat to let himself be seen, and waved to the crowd that had gathered to watch.

'It is Hat-Neb! The overseer of works has returned!'

'Behold his fine new boat!'

Willing hands reached out for ropes as the boat was manoeuvred into position, and a wide plank ladder was winched up to the deck. Hat-Neb called to Killer, and picked up the hunting cat. Then, with great dignity, he began to disembark. But halfway down, he stopped and swayed. Isis heard a murmur ripple through the crowd. He righted himself, and clutched the cat to his chest. One slow step at a time, he reached the docks.

The sound of a whip cracked through the air, and horses' hooves thudded on the hard earth of the riverside. A gilded chariot came into view, pulled by two cantering horses, each with an ostrich plume attached to its head. The crowd parted, and the chariot came to a halt by Hat-Neb's side. He looked back up at the boat.

'Come, Tutmose!' he called.

The doctor descended to join the overseer, raising a

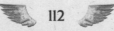

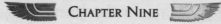

hand to the crowd as he made his way to the chariot. The two men climbed on board behind the driver, and Isis stared down at them. Was Hat-Neb going to leave them, just like that? It seemed that he was. The overseer waved up to Nebo.

'Stand guard!' he called. 'I will send men to help you unload!'

The chariot driver cracked his whip, and the horses set off through the crowd in a cloud of dust. There were just the crew, the dance troupe and Nebo left on board.

Nebo turned to Kerem. 'You take the sick men off,' he said, jerking his head in the direction of the injured crew. 'And then you follow.'

Kerem did not protest. The crowd ogled eagerly as the injured men were helped down the plank, their bandages still bloody and one man's arm dangling uselessly. Kerem was the last to go.

Sheri and Kia looked at Nebo, clearly confused.

'Now what?' exclaimed Kia. 'Who is going to carry our belongings off the boat? And what about our payment?'

'You go free when the boat unloaded. Your payment . . .' Nebo shrugged. 'This nothing to do with me.'

Kia's mouth dropped open. 'What do you mean, nothing?' She folded her arms. 'You've no authority

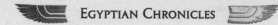
to pay us what we're owed?'

'No.' The Nubian's voice was remote.

'And that's it? You are not going to help us?'

Another shrug. Sheri and Kia exchanged furious glances. Then a shout came from below, and six strong servants appeared up the ladder. They set to work diligently, running up and down the plank to unload Hat-Neb's sacks of grain, his caskets and his statues. In no time at all, the hold was empty. The men moved on to the cabin.

'What do we do with these?' asked one of them, pointing to the troupe's belongings.

Nebo nodded his head towards the shore. 'Take them down and leave them on the harbour.'

'Be careful with them!' cried Sheri, as the men grabbed their fragile lyres and lutes. The men grinned at each other, and carried on as before.

It was then that Isis realised the truth. They had survived this dreadful journey, but now they were stuck. They would be left at the riverside, with no payment, and no means of returning to Waset.

Hopi watched as the last of Hat-Neb's pack donkeys disappeared up the road. Sheri and Kia were enraged. Hopi had never seen them so angry. The five of them stood on the harbour with their little pile of

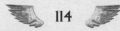

belongings. Locals stared at them curiously – a dance and music troupe with nowhere to go.

'I can't believe it. I simply can't believe it. In all my years of performing I have never, ever been treated like this.' Kia began striding up and down, her arms folded. 'There must be something we can do. *Something* –'

'Such men are above the law,' said Sheri bitterly.

'This is not the way of Egypt. This is not the way of *ma'at*,' fumed Kia.

But Hopi had one eye on the crew. 'There *is* something we can do,' he announced. 'And I must do it, for I have given my word, and there will be big trouble if I do not.'

The two musicians swung around to stare at him. 'Hopi! You have caused enough trouble on this trip,' began Kia. 'I suppose you will produce some kind of –'

'Wait, sister. Calm yourself,' said Sheri. 'Let us hear what he has to say.'

The crew were watching them. What Hopi knew, and the women did not, was that their danger was far from over. They might have escaped Hat-Neb and Nebo, but now Kerem and his men wanted results. It was noon, and the sun was beating down harshly. Hopi pointed towards a large, shady fig tree close by.

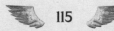

'Let's sit under this tree,' he said. 'And I will explain.'

Kia looked suspicious, but Sheri picked up her lyre. The five of them carried their belongings to the shadow of the tree and spread out some reed matting.

'So,' said Sheri, making herself comfortable. 'Tell us, Hopi. What is it that you must do?'

Hopi took a deep breath. 'I have to go and find Tutmose.'

'But he went with Hat-Neb,' said Mut.

'Yes. But he has an important task to finish, and he has lost what he needs to do so.' Hopi glanced over to the crew as he spoke. They had bought some strips of roasted meat from a local vendor, and were sitting eating it. 'I have promised the crew that they will receive their gold,' he said. 'And I'm quite sure that Tutmose will help me to get it.'

'What! Receive their . . . but how?' exclaimed Sheri. 'What is this task that Tutmose must finish?'

Hopi leaned forward. 'Tutmose may be a doctor,' he said in a low voice, 'but he is also an assassin. And he was supposed to murder Hat-Neb.'

There was a shocked silence. Quietly, Hopi reached for his bag.

'So what has he lost?' asked Isis.

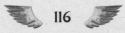

Hopi smiled. 'It is here,' he said. He delved into his bag, and brought out the pouch he had found in the hold – the pouch full of Tutmose's poisons.

Isis thought of Hat-Neb sweating and suffering under the sun. Hat-Neb toppling and collapsing on their trip to the marshes. Hat-Neb vomiting over the side of the fishing boat. Hat-Neb waking up in the night, choking and coughing. And Tutmose . . . Tutmose offering treatment. Tutmose creeping around at night. Tutmose with Hat-Neb's fan, working his magic under the cover of darkness. Now, it all made sense.

'But why didn't he succeed sooner?' Sheri looked at the array of bottles and potions. 'There is surely enough to kill twenty men here.'

'I'm not sure,' said Hopi. 'I think it was to make it look natural. Hat-Neb was becoming sick, but he didn't want to believe it. He was happy to blame his wine. That suited Tutmose very well.'

'How dreadful,' murmured Sheri.

Isis was still thinking. 'So who were the men who attacked us?' she asked. 'They wanted to kill Hat-Neb, too, didn't they?'

'Yes,' said Hopi. 'There are many men who would like to see Hat-Neb dead. From what I have seen, he has caused a great deal of misery. But Tutmose didn't

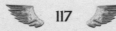

want the barge men to do it, because they would have had to kill our crew first. Then we'd all have been stuck.'

'And I suppose he's being paid by someone to do the job himself,' said Sheri thoughtfully. 'I can see that the viper might have been useful to him.'

Hopi nodded. 'He wanted some of its venom for his collection.' He began packing the poisons back into his bag. 'So, as I said, I need to find him. He wants these poisons back, but he won't get them unless he helps us.'

'But our payment doesn't matter that much, Hopi! This trip has been quite dangerous enough,' exclaimed Sheri. 'We have plenty of things we can sell.'

'Oh yes. I don't want that collar Hat-Neb gave me,' said Isis. 'We can –'

'You've forgotten something,' Hopi interrupted her. 'Look over there.'

Isis looked. The crew had finished eating. Kerem was getting to his feet, and heading in their direction. And from the deep frown that furrowed his brow, Isis could see he meant business.

'The crew have suffered greatly. They want their gold,' said Hopi. 'They did as I asked last night. Now I must keep my side of the bargain.'

Sheri and Kia exchanged worried glances, but Isis

touched Hopi's arm. 'Wherever you're going, I'm coming with you,' she declared. 'I won't let you go alone.'

The troupe looked up as Kerem stopped in front of them. His regard was cold and distant, and his stance was tinged with menace. 'So,' he said, 'will our priest fulfil his promise?'

Hopi got to his feet, leaving his bag on the ground with Sheri and Kia. 'I will do my best. I am leaving now,' he said. 'And my sister is coming with me. Come on, Isis, let's go.'

The temple site was situated a short distance away from the river. Hopi and Isis followed a well-trodden road from the harbour, blending in with the stream of people who bustled along it.

'Listen to everyone,' muttered Hopi. 'Try to catch anything that might be helpful. Anything about the temple, or doctors, overseers, Nubians, mercenaries . . .'

Isis nodded. 'I'm good at that sort of thing.'

It was true. Isis had a knack for eavesdropping and disappearing into shadows. Her nimble body could wriggle in and out of very awkward places. Hopi was glad that she was with him. He didn't like to admit it, but he was afraid. They might never find Tutmose, and this town was crawling with men under the power of Hat-Neb.

They turned a corner, and the temple came into view. It was built on higher ground, safe from the flood water, and although it wasn't yet finished, it was an amazing sight. Massive ramps had been constructed on which hundreds of men toiled. Some of the walls had been completed, so that draughtsmen, sculptors and painters were the ones at work here, drawing and chipping with chisels to extol the gods and the king. On the other side, men were still hauling enormous limestone blocks up the ramps to finish the building work.

They overtook a group of labourers trudging slowly towards the site carrying baskets of gravel on their bare shoulders.

'Did you hear that?' whispered Isis.

'No. What?'

'They were saying *he's back*,' said Isis. 'Hopi, they could be talking about Hat-Neb! Should we go and ask them?'

Hopi hesitated. Many men were bound to know of the overseer's return. 'We need something more useful,' he said. 'We mustn't draw attention to ourselves unless we have to.'

They were already attracting stares; they needed an excuse to be this close to the temple. Hopi spotted an old man tottering along with a basket of

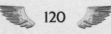

pomegranates on his head, and grabbed Isis by the hand.

'Come on,' he said. 'Let's pretend to be with him.'

They soon caught up with the vendor, who was stooped under the weight of his basket.

'May we help you?' Isis offered, with a pretty smile.

The man's watery eyes looked at them with distrust. 'I know your sort,' he grumbled.

'No, no,' said Isis. 'We don't want to steal your fruit. You are tired. Why don't you sit and rest, while we sell the fruit for you?'

'What are you after?' demanded the vendor.

'A pomegranate each,' responded Hopi quickly.

The man put down his basket and flopped to the ground. 'I'll try you out,' he said, and handed them each some fruit.

'Pomegranates!' sang Isis, skipping up to one man after another. 'Lovely, big, fresh pomegranates!'

'I have a small packet of salt here,' offered a scribe. 'How many will that buy?'

'I'll check.' Isis scampered back to the old man.

Hopi let Isis do most of the work. She was much better at it than him. He watched his sister as she danced around, charming men into buying more pomegranates than they wanted, for goods they had

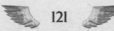

not meant to sell. The vendor was delighted. But the day was wearing on, and they were no closer to solving their problem.

Then Hopi saw him: Tutmose, approaching the site on foot.

'Isis!' he called urgently.

She spun around. Hopi ducked down behind a broken limestone block, and beckoned her. Isis handed over two pomegranates to a deputy overseer, and dived around the block to join her brother.

Tutmose walked through the site uncertainly, as though it was unfamiliar to him. He looked around, stopped and craned his neck. At last, he saw what he was looking for. With more purpose in his stride, he walked straight to their last customer – the deputy overseer, who was already peeling a pomegranate.

The deputy looked shocked to see Tutmose. 'What are you doing here?' he demanded.

He took the doctor's arm and steered him into the shade of an acacia tree, dangerously close to the limestone block. Hopi and Isis shuffled along hurriedly, then stayed still and listened.

'I needed to see you.' The doctor's voice was urgent.

'You are putting us both at risk. And I hear that you have failed.'

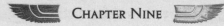

'The task is still in hand.' Tutmose sounded flustered. 'But there have been problems. Setbacks. I have come to say that I need more time.'

'More time!' The deputy sounded incredulous. 'You have had an entire trip down the Nile –'

'Yes, yes, but it is not easy. We must not arouse suspicion. I am a respected physician. Everyone must believe he died of natural causes.'

'I thought that was your speciality,' said the deputy. 'That's what I was told. But at this rate, he will die of natural causes without any help from you!'

'Hush, hush,' Tutmose soothed him. 'I am still a guest in his house. I have promised to cure his various . . . problems. He wishes to be fit and well before he returns to the building site.'

'Small mercies,' muttered the deputy. 'Well, let me know when the task is completed.'

'Indeed. It is well under way, I can assure you. And on the basis of that, I wonder if there might be an advance – a small advance – on my payment . . .'

The deputy gave a cracked laugh. 'What do you take me for?' he exclaimed. 'You know the terms of our agreement perfectly well.'

'Yes, yes . . .' The doctor was floundering. 'It is just that . . . just that . . . I need supplies . . . I have run out of so many of my potions . . .'

'Here, have a pomegranate,' said the deputy, his voice hard. 'That is all you will receive from me until you can tell me the job is done.'

Isis paid the pomegranate vendor the handful of beads that the deputy had given her. 'We have to go now,' she told him. Hopi was fast disappearing down the road.

'A thousand blessings be upon you!' cried the old man, handing her two of his best ripe fruits. Isis thanked him, and hurried after her brother.

Tutmose was heading for the town. He stomped along in a fury, swearing at anyone who got in his way. Isis and Hopi kept at a distance, but were careful not to lose sight of him. They were already winding through narrow streets, and the doctor walked fast.

Hopi struggled to keep up. 'We must find a safe place to speak to him,' he gasped. 'Where no one will see.'

'I'll go and offer him these pomegranates,' suggested Isis. 'No one will suspect a thing. Catch me up.'

She skipped off, weaving in and out of people, donkeys and ducks. She picked her moment carefully, stopping Tutmose just at the entrance to a dim alleyway.

'Fresh pomegranates!' she sang loudly, jogging the

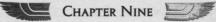

doctor's elbow.

He tutted impatiently, and snatched his elbow away. Then he saw that it was Isis. '*You*,' he scowled. 'What do you think you're doing?'

Isis smiled and batted her eyelashes. 'Why, this is only fresh fruit, sir!' she said. 'Please, come here so that we can discuss it.' And she stepped into the alleyway.

Tutmose looked up and down the street, then reached out to grab Isis by the arm. She was too quick for him, and danced out of the way.

'Where's that brother of yours?' he snapped. 'I'll murder the pair of you.'

'Yes, I'm sure you'd like to try.' Hopi appeared behind him, blocking the alleyway. 'But you might find it difficult without any of your poisons.'

Tutmose spun on his heel, then back at Isis. He was trapped.

Hopi looked levelly at the doctor. 'You thought you'd left us behind, didn't you?' he said. 'Well, we have a problem. We can't leave until we've been paid. We can't afford the ferry back to Waset.'

'And what do you expect me to do about it? I'm not your employer. Now let me go –' Tutmose tried to push past Hopi, but Isis grabbed his linen kilt and yanked it hard. The doctor snatched it back hastily as

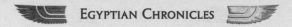

it began to unravel, and hoisted it up around his waist.

'We expect you to help us – and the crew, too.' Hopi folded his arms. 'We weren't the only ones left stranded at the harbour.'

Tutmose gave a nervous laugh. 'The crew? That rabble can take care of themselves. They won't get any help from me.'

'Oh?' Hopi raised an eyebrow. 'And what if we told Hat-Neb that you are trying to poison him? We could tell him who's employed you to do it, while we're there.'

The doctor's mouth dropped open. 'You couldn't – you can't –' he stuttered. 'You have no idea what you're talking about!'

'I do, actually,' said Hopi quietly. 'We overheard everything that you said to the deputy overseer at the temple site. He's not very happy with you, is he? It's such a shame that you've lost your poisons.'

Tutmose glared at Hopi bitterly. 'I knew you'd taken them, you little thief.'

'It sounds as though you need them back.'

The doctor leaned back against the alley wall, and sighed. 'Very well,' he said. 'What do you want me to do?'

CHAPTER TEN

The atmosphere at the harbour was uneasy. Kerem and his men had formed a circle around Sheri, Kia and Mut, who were trying hard to hide their fear. Hopi hurried up with Isis, breathless.

'Everything is in place,' he announced. 'We shall all receive our payment.'

'Hopi! That's wonderful,' exclaimed Sheri, rising to her feet and kissing him on the cheek.

But Kerem looked suspicious. 'How?' he asked. 'You mean the crew also?'

'Yes,' Hopi assured him. 'The only problem is this: we shall have to collect it ourselves.'

'Collect it? You mean Hat-Neb has agreed to pay after all?' Sheri sounded delighted.

'Not exactly. It's a bit more complicated than that.' Hopi leaned against the broad trunk of the

 127

fig tree, nursing his weary leg.

'He has struck a deal with Tutmose,' announced Isis. 'It's very clever. We'll all be on our way back to Waset before Hat-Neb has even woken up.'

Kia frowned. 'What do you mean, woken up? Why is he asleep?'

'He isn't. Not yet. But he will be tonight. And that is when we shall collect our payment,' said Hopi. 'Tutmose won't risk being caught red-handed, but he has agreed to drug Hat-Neb's guards. I will go to Hat-Neb's house with Isis. We shall take our payment from his stores. And then we shall leave. The crew may stay here if they wish, but we can take the dawn boat to Waset.'

'You mean – *steal* from him?' Kia sounded horrified.

'We shall take what is rightfully ours,' said Hopi. 'How is that stealing?'

No one replied to that. Silence fell. Kerem turned away, and began to stride up and down. He stared out at the Nile for a while. Then he marched back, and stood in front of Hopi.

'Why does Tutmose help us?' he asked. 'Why do you trust this man?'

'I don't trust him,' said Hopi. 'But I have his pouch of poisons, and he needs it back. Such poisons are

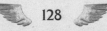

difficult to come by and it would take him a long time to replace them. Anyway, he is very afraid, for we have the power to betray him.'

'We must come with you to the house of Hat-Neb,' said Kerem.

Hopi shook his head. He had thought it all through. 'No. It would be better if you stay and guard the poisons. Tutmose may try to trick us, so I want to leave them here. He can come and collect them afterwards. Anyway, only Isis will enter the house.'

'Isis! No!' said Sheri. 'I can't allow it! Hopi, she could be killed! How can you even think of such a thing?'

Hopi looked at his sister. Going into the house alone had been her idea. She could move faster than anyone else, and silently, too. He was afraid for her, but proud at the same time.

'It's better this way,' he said. 'I will only slow her down.'

Isis nodded. 'I know I can do it,' she said quietly. 'I am quick and small. I can outrun Tutmose any day.'

'But, Isis, there may be more guards. What if they come from behind . . .' Sheri was distraught.

'Look around you, Sheri.' Hopi's voice was sharp.

The crew were growing impatient, tired of all the talking. They spoke to Kerem, and he snapped

something back. Sheri and Kia looked nervously at their sharpened daggers and unkempt hair.

Isis followed their gaze. 'You see,' she said. 'We have little choice.'

Hat-Neb's mansion was outside the town, surrounded by a high whitewashed wall. Isis and Hopi tiptoed along a track lined with palm trees and lush vegetation. The air throbbed with the sound of crickets and croaking frogs.

'The gate's open,' whispered Isis. 'You stay here.'

Hopi stepped off the track. Isis slipped forward, keeping to the shadows. Maybe Tutmose would have set a trap for her, after all. The gate creaked, and Isis jumped. She waited, but there was nothing except the wind rustling the palm fronds. She reached the edge of the wall and began to creep forward on all fours.

Something grunted, close by. Isis froze. Another grunt, followed by a deep, whistling sigh. She breathed out in relief. It was the sound of snoring. So the guards *were* asleep. Isis spotted the guard just outside the gate, his head lolling against the wall. Isis swallowed. She would have to step over his legs to go through the gate. She wiped her hands on her linen dress and looked back up the track, but Hopi had melted into the darkness. She was on her own. She

placed one foot on the other side of the guard's legs and peered into the grounds.

Another guard was lying on the other side of the gate. He, too, was fast asleep. Isis pushed the gate open just enough for her slender body to slip through. The hinges squealed, and her mouth went dry. But the guards slept on, and Isis found herself inside the gardens of Hat-Neb's magnificent house.

The gardens were beautiful. In the moonlight, Isis saw a big pond with lotus flowers floating on its surface, the water rippling gently. The scent from herbs and the blossoms of shrubs filled the air. For a second, Isis felt a pang of sadness that the man who owned all this had turned out to be so horrible.

She pushed the thought away and tiptoed down a path that led towards the house. It wound between dark bushes, and she entered the blackness with her eyes wide, straining to see. She stopped. Something was there. Some*one* was there, in front of her, shifting out of the shadows. Isis yelped in terror.

'Don't worry,' murmured a voice. It was Tutmose.

Shaking, Isis said nothing.

The doctor moved closer, and spoke in her ear, 'You can enter the house by the side door, on the left ahead of you. What you seek is in a room to the right along the corridor. I will wait for you outside the grounds.'

Isis found her voice. 'Hopi is already there,' she whispered. 'Once I have come back out safely, we shall take you to collect your poisons.'

Tutmose melted back into the shadows, and Isis swallowed. *This is it*, she thought to herself, and hurried on towards the house.

Everything was as Tutmose said it would be. Isis found the door open, and slipped inside. All was silent. Isis listened, and heard the distant rhythm of Hat-Neb's snores, somewhere above. She wondered where Nebo might be, and her courage almost failed her. But then she drove herself on. This would soon be over.

With no moonlight to help her, she groped her way along the corridor until her fingers came to a doorway on her right. She stopped to listen again. Still nothing. Holding her breath, Isis entered the cold, quiet room. Moonlight filtered through the clerestory windows that ran around the top, and she gazed on an extraordinary sight. The room was stacked with precious goods: no ornate objects of great craftsmanship, but many of the elements that were used to make them. There were open caskets of precious stones – carnelian, turquoise, jade, lapis lazuli and slabs of creamy alabaster; planks of the finest cedar propped up against the wall; on the floor, a pile of

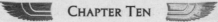

leopard skins of the sort worn by priests. Filling the air was the heavy scent of incense; Isis caught wafts of cinnamon, frankincense and myrrh, and saw a row of priceless oils and ointments. It was hard to take it all in.

Then she came to her senses. She had come for gold; that was what she must find. She stepped further into the room, bewildered. She ran her hand along the caskets of precious stones, picked up a handful of carnelian pieces, then let them drop from her fingers.

'Perhaps I can help you.'

Isis froze, her hand still hovering over the casket of carnelian. Her heart thudded against her chest. For a second, she closed her eyes. It had happened. She had been caught.

She let her hand drop, and turned round to face Nebo. The fan-bearer stood in the doorway, his massive frame quite clear in the glimmering moonlight.

'What are you doing here?' he asked.

'I . . . I came to take our payment. Ours, and that of the crew.'

'And how did you get past the guards?'

Isis licked her lips. 'I can't tell you that.'

Seconds ticked past. Isis expected Nebo to reach out and grab her. She slid her eyes around the room,

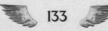

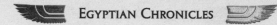

looking for an escape, but there was nowhere for her to go. She was trapped.

'So what did they tell you to take?' Nebo asked.

Isis stared at him. What difference did it make now? She shrugged. 'Gold for the crew. That is what they were promised. We were to be paid to the value of eight *debens* of copper, so I was going to take a small piece of gold for us, too. If I could find some.'

'I show you.' Nebo pointed to a small casket in the far corner.

Isis couldn't believe it. What was he doing? Was he playing games with her? She tried to move her feet, but they felt stuck to the floor.

'Go!' ordered the Nubian. 'The gold is there!'

But Isis still couldn't move. All she could think of was how his dagger had felt, when its cold, sharp point had touched her throat.

'You would have killed me, on the boat,' she said. She tried to move her feet again, and this time they obeyed. Still keeping her eyes on Nebo's face, she moved slowly to the casket in the corner.

'Yes,' said Nebo. 'I would have killed you.'

'So why don't you just kill me now?' Isis put her hand on the casket and lifted the lid. She looked away from the fan-bearer to see what lay inside, and gasped. The casket was full of gold in all its forms –

rough nuggets fresh from the mines, small beaten bars, strips of gold wire . . .

A heavy hand landed on her shoulder. She jumped, and looked up into Nebo's face.

'Do you have a bag?' he asked.

With a trembling finger, Isis pointed to the pouch that she had slung around her waist.

'Take what you are owed.'

Isis was bewildered, terrified. Her mouth dry, she counted out what she guessed was about the right amount of gold, and placed it in her pouch.

'Now go.' Nebo took his hand off her shoulder.

This wasn't right. It had to be a trick. Isis looked up at Nebo distrustfully. 'Why are you doing this?' she whispered.

'Because of . . . because, little Isis, you make me think of my . . .' Nebo's voice shook with emotion. He stopped himself and stood a little straighter. 'Hat-Neb does not know you are here.'

'But he is in the house. I heard him . . .'

Nebo said nothing. Isis came to her senses. If he was giving her a chance, she must take it. She ran a few light steps to the door. The fan-bearer did not stop her.

On the threshold, she looked back. 'Who will take the blame, when he finds out?'

Nebo shook his head. 'He will never find out.'

He and Isis looked at each other, and Isis understood.

'He is dying?'

'Yes.'

Isis knew she should have left already, but she wanted to ask one last question. 'What will you do when he has gone?'

Almost imperceptibly, Nebo flexed his muscles, and in the pale light, Isis saw the life die in his eyes. 'There is always work for a man who will kill anything,' he said.

Isis felt a chill run down her spine. With a little cry, she turned away, and fled down the corridor into the night.

The contest was in full swing. Pairs of boys fought to overbalance each other in their little boats, while the villagers laughed and cheered. Hopi watched as one boy lost his balance and fell into the water. He surfaced, spluttering and laughing, and pulled himself back on to his wobbling craft.

'I'd love to have a go at that, wouldn't you?' said Mut wistfully.

'No thanks,' replied Isis. 'I don't mind the river as much as I used to, but I don't like it *that* much!'

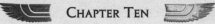

Hopi shielded his eyes from the sun as the passenger boat moved on downriver, beyond the village games. They had passed the marshes where Isis and Mut had gone hunting, and were well on their way back to Waset. He was feeling impatient. There was so much to tell Menna – and so much to ask him, too.

But the boat was slowing down. It looked as though it was pulling in to the bank – again. Hopi sighed. Passenger boats always took for ever to get anywhere. They were laden high with people's belongings, merchandise, even their livestock. Passengers got on and off at inconvenient places, made the boat wait for hobbling relatives or while they carried out a transaction . . .

He wondered what they were stopping for this time. Now they had passed the village, they were in the middle of nowhere. Then he noticed that a group of women at the back were shouting, pointing and hurriedly shifting their possessions. Hopi tutted. The boat must be leaking, and worse than usual.

The captain guided the long vessel towards a shallow bank, where a clump of doum palms rose up against a barren hillside. Hopi gave a start. He recognised this spot. It was exactly where they had been attacked by the barge crew.

'Everyone out!' called the captain cheerfully. 'Relax

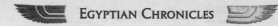

for a while. I'll soon have it fixed. Just needs a bit of plugging up.'

With a good deal of grumbling, the passengers disembarked, splashing to the shore with their goods on their shoulders, to sit in the shade of the palms. Mut, Isis and Hopi helped Sheri and Kia to carry their instruments to safety, then Hopi grabbed Isis by the hand.

'Come with me,' he said. 'There's something I want to show you.'

He began to walk up the hillside with its view of the river. Isis followed him, skipping lightly from rock to rock as they climbed. They reached the brow of the hill, and Hopi flopped on to the dry ground.

Isis sat down next to him. They surveyed the riverbank below, and the wind billowing the sail of a passing pleasure boat. Hopi was reaching for his bag when Isis spoke.

'Hopi,' she said, 'there's something I want to say.'

'Oh?' Hopi looked at her quickly. She sounded serious.

Isis studied her fingers. 'It's just that . . . you were right about Hat-Neb,' she said. 'And I'm sorry.'

Hopi smiled. His sister might be impulsive, but she was always very fair. 'And Nebo?' he asked.

Isis frowned. 'I was wrong about him, too,' she

said. 'But it's funny. Some bad people have good bits, too.'

'And the other way round,' agreed Hopi. He sighed. 'Well, the same goes for Tutmose. I was wrong about him.'

'We were both wrong, and neither of us wanted to see it. It was horrible,' said Isis. 'And that's what I've been thinking about. I never want to disagree with you again. Not like that. Never, never, never.'

Hopi grinned. 'Maybe we won't be able to help it.'

'We *have* to help it.' Isis sounded very determined. 'I won't let it happen again. Not if you won't.'

'Sounds fair to me,' said Hopi.

Isis smiled. 'Good.'

They turned their faces to the breeze for a moment, and listened to the voices drifting up from between the swaying doum palms.

'Was this what you wanted to show me?' asked Isis. 'The view?'

'Oh! No. I nearly forgot,' said Hopi. 'This is where I caught the horned viper. Well, not far from here.' And he reached again for his basket.

'You still have it!' exclaimed Isis.

'Of course. There hasn't been anywhere to release it,' said Hopi.

He lifted the lid off the papyrus basket, and placed

it on its side so that the snake could escape. Together, they watched as it slithered out, testing the air with its tongue. The bulge of the rat inside it had gone down, and it moved steadily up towards a cluster of rocks.

'Welcome home,' murmured Hopi.

The viper passed the rocks, its tongue still flicking. It reached a patch of golden dune that stretched out to the desert beyond, and paused for a moment. Then, with deft sideways movements, it vanished beneath the sand.

CAST OF CHARACTERS

CHRONICLE CHARACTERS

Hopi The thirteen-year-old brother of Isis. Ever since surviving the bite of a crocodile in the attack that killed their parents, Hopi has had a fascination with dangerous creatures, particularly snakes and scorpions. He is training to be a priest of Serqet, which will qualify him to treat bites and stings.

Isis The eleven-year-old sister of Hopi. She is a talented dancer and performs regularly with Nefert and Paneb's troupe. Her dance partner is Mut.

Mut The eleven-year-old daughter of Paneb and Nefert, and dance partner to Isis.

Paneb Husband of Nefert, father of Mut, Ramose and Kha, and the head of the household where Isis and Hopi live. He organises bookings for the dance and music troupe.

Nefert Wife of Paneb, mother of Mut, Ramose and Kha, and sister of Sheri and Kia. She plays the lute and is head of the dance and music troupe.

Sheri One of Nefert's widowed sisters, and a musician

in the troupe. She has a particularly loving nature.

Kia   The second of Nefert's widowed sisters, also a musician living with the troupe. She is slightly more cold and distant than Sheri, but is hardworking and practical.

Ramose   Eldest son of Nefert and Paneb, aged five. Mut's brother.

Kha   Younger son of Nefert and Paneb, aged two. Mut's brother.

Menna   Hopi's tutor, and a priest of Serqet in the town of Waset. (A priest of Serqet was someone who treated snake bites and scorpion stings.)

OTHER CHARACTERS IN THIS STORY

Hat-Neb   A powerful overseer of public works. He is currently the overseer at the new temple being built for the god Horus in Djeba. He has a reputation for great cruelty.

Nebo   Hat-Neb's fan-bearer and guard. He is from Nubia, the area just to the south of Egypt, and part of the ancient Egyptian empire.

Tutmose   A qualified doctor who has worked in the royal court, but now treats wealthy men.

Kerem   The head of a group of Sea People sailors, who hire themselves out to work on boats on the Nile. They also act as mercenaries, which means they will fight for whoever pays them.

Senmut   The leader of a group of rowers who know of Hat-Neb's reputation.

Ipuy   A young scribe who works at the temple site in Djeba.

MAP OF ANCIENT EGYPT

MEDITERRANEAN SEA

The Nile Delta

Per Ramesses
(A New Kingdom
capital city)

Old Kingdom
Pyramids

Natron salt
found here

The Red land
(Desert)

The Red land
(Desert)

The River Nile

RED SEA

The Great
Place
(The Valley of
the Kings)

Waset
(Luxor)

Set Maat
(Deir el Medina)

Djeba
(Edfu)

N
W — E
S

NUBIA

Granite and
gold mines
found here

FASCINATING FACT FILE ABOUT ANCIENT EGYPT

THE WORLD OF ISIS AND HOPI

The stories of Isis and Hopi are based in ancient Egypt over 3,000 years ago, during a time known as the New Kingdom. They happen around 1200–1150 BC, in the last great period of Egyptian history. This is about a thousand years after the Old Kingdom, when the pyramids were built. Waset, the town in which Isis and Hopi live, had recently been the capital of Egypt, with an enormous temple complex dedicated to the god Amun. By 1200 BC, the capital had been moved further north again, but Waset was still very important. Kings were still buried in the Valley of the Kings on the west bank, and the priests of Amun were rich and powerful. Today, Waset is known as Luxor; in books about ancient Egypt, it is often referred to by the Greek name of Thebes.

146

A Little Bit about Horned Vipers

The snake that Hopi finds in this book is a desert horned viper, also called the Sahara horned viper. These snakes have a sandy-coloured body with brown blotches, a wide, triangular head, and two big scales that stick up behind the eyes to create 'horns'.

Horned vipers are desert snakes. They tend to live in dry river beds and among sand and rocks. They are usually nocturnal – in other words, they are active and do their hunting at night. During the day, they bury themselves in sand or hide somewhere shady, though they are sometimes seen basking in the sun. They move by 'sidewinding', which means pressing part of their body down while throwing another part sideways and forwards. This leaves an unmistakable track in soft sand.

As venomous snakes go, horned vipers are not very aggressive – but when they strike, they strike fast. Hopi's viper would have had no problem catching a rat in the hold! The bite of a horned viper is dangerous, but it does not often kill people.

When it is cornered, a horned viper sometimes curls into C-shaped coils and rubs its scales together

as a warning. This makes a rasping, hissing sound. What's interesting is that the ancient Egyptian hiero- glyph for a horned viper is also the letter 'f'. People now think that this might be because of the sound the snake makes with its coils: *fffff*.

BOATS AND THE RIVER NILE

The ancient Egyptians didn't bother building lots of roads, because the River Nile was like a big highway running from one end of Egypt to the other. Away from the Nile, there was only desert, where no one wanted to go. Because the Nile flooded every year, covering the fields, roads close to the river got washed away. So to travel up and down the length of Egypt, people used boats.

The Nile flows from south to north, emptying out into the Mediterranean Sea. Luckily, the wind in Egypt usually blows in the opposite direction, from north to south. So to travel north, boats could go with the current, often with the help of oars. To travel south, boats had sails to catch the wind and carry them against the current. Because of this, the hiero- glyph that meant 'travel north' was a picture of a boat without a sail, and the hieroglyph for 'travel south' was a picture of a boat with a sail.

For pottering around close to home, fishing or hunting in the marshes, people made little boats out of papyrus reeds bundled together. By the New Kingdom, some of these would have been made of wood instead.

For religious ceremonies and to carry the king, there were elegant, brightly painted boats that we now call *barques*. These were slender boats with a beautifully carved prow. The Egyptians believed that the sun god Re sailed across the sky in a barque every day. Wealthy people, like Hat-Neb in the story, might own pleasure boats built of wood. Like barques, these would have been brightly painted, with a cabin to keep the owner sheltered from the sun.

There were big rowing boats to carry cargoes, and massive barges to carry very heavy loads, like blocks of stone. These barges were so large that they had to be towed by smaller boats, like the one in the story.

EGYPT'S TEMPLES

Temples were central to religion in ancient Egypt. They were built for the glory of the gods and king, and only priests and priestesses could enter the inner areas. Ordinary people had to stay outside, but they could still make offerings and pray to the gods, using the priests and scribes attached to the temples as go-betweens.

There were two main kinds of temple – cult temples and mortuary temples. Cult temples were for the worship of a particular god, like Sobek or Amun. The temple being built in the book is a cult temple dedicated to the god Horus, in a place that is now called Edfu. The ancient name for the temple site was Djeba, and there was a temple there from Old Kingdom times. Kings in the New Kingdom added to this temple to make it more impressive, but it's difficult to say exactly how much. This is because from 237 BC onwards, the Ptolomies (Greek invaders) built a big new temple on the same site. You can still visit this temple today.

Mortuary temples were for the worship of a dead king. For this reason, they were usually built on the west bank – the Kingdom of the Dead – not too far from the tombs where the kings were buried.

Both cult and mortuary temples were huge, amazing buildings. Many of them have survived, and you can still see the massive walls, columns and statues, and the hieroglyphs that were carved everywhere. It's a little bit harder to imagine the bright colours that the temples were painted in.

THE SEA PEOPLE

The crew of Hat-Neb's boat are 'Sea People' who have settled in Egypt. No one is really sure who these people were or where they came from, but they gave some of the New Kingdom kings a lot of bother. Waves of Sea People attacked Egypt along the north coast during the reign of the great king Ramesses II (who reigned from approximately 1279–1212 BC), but Ramesses defeated them, taking many captives. Later, these captives formed part of the Egyptian army and helped to fight other enemies, so some of the Sea People would have made Egypt their home.

About a century later, during the reign of Ramesses III (approximately 1186–1154 BC), there was another wave of Sea People attacks. Again, the Egyptians defeated and killed many of them. But there would have been captives, too, who settled in Egypt.

In this story, I have put together their knowledge of boats and the role that they played as mercenaries, and imagined that some of them would have hired themselves out as guards and sailors on the Nile.

NUBIANS

Nubia is a region that lies in the south of Egypt and on into Sudan. For much of ancient Egyptian history, it formed part of the Egyptian empire and was a very important source of gold – in fact, 'Nubia' means 'Land of Gold'. But later on in its history, Egypt was conquered by Nubia, and had Nubian pharaohs for almost a hundred years (approximately 747–656 BC).

Nubians were portrayed in statues and wall paintings with much darker skin than Egyptians. They were famous for their fierce fighting skills, especially with bows and arrows – another ancient name for Nubia, 'Ta-Seti', meant 'Land of the Bow'. Egyptian kings often hired Nubian soldiers to fight alongside Egyptian regiments.

GODS AND GODDESSES

Ancient Egyptian religion was very complicated. There wasn't just one god, but hundreds, each symbolising something different. Many of them were linked to a particular animal or plant. The Egyptians believed that their king or pharaoh was one of the gods, too.

Not everyone worshipped the same gods. It would have been very difficult to worship all of them, because there were so many. Some gods were more important than others, and some places had special gods of their own. People would have had their favourites depending on where they lived and what they did.

These are some of the most important gods of the New Kingdom, and all the special ones that are mentioned in this book.

Amun The great god of Waset (Thebes), a creator god and god of the air. When Waset became very powerful in the New Kingdom, he was combined with the sun god Re and became **Amun-Re**. He was shown with tall feathers on his head, or with a ram's head.

Anubis The god of mummies and embalming. He was usually shown with a jackal's head.

Apep The great snake god of darkness, chaos and evil. He was usually shown as an enormous serpent, but sometimes as a crocodile or even a dragon.

Bes A god who was worshipped in people's homes, rather than at shrines and temples. He was shown as a bearded dwarf, often with his tongue sticking out, and was believed to protect people's houses, pregnant women and children.

Hapi The god of the Nile, specifically the Nile flood that happened every year. Although he was a male god, he was shown with large breasts because he represented fertility.

Hathor A goddess of fertility, love, music and dancing. She was usually shown as a cow, or a woman with a cow's head, or a woman with a cow's ears and horns.

Horus The falcon-headed king of the gods, who fought and won a battle with his evil uncle Seth. The reigning king of Egypt was believed to be the embodiment of Horus. His cult temple was at Djeba (Edfu).

Isis The mother of Horus and wife of Osiris, the goddess of motherhood and royal protection. She was associated with the goddess Hathor.

Khepri The scarab god, the god of the rising sun. It was believed that he pushed the sun up every morning in the same way that a scarab pushes its ball of dung.

Khonsu The moon god of Waset, worshipped in the great temple complex there. He was the adopted son of Mut.

Mut The great mother-goddess of Waset, worshipped with Amun and Khonsu. Because Waset is often called Thebes, these three are known as the 'Theban Triad'.

Osiris Husband of Isis, father of Horus and brother of the evil god Seth. He was the king of the underworld, so he was usually shown as a mummy.

Re (or **Ra**) The sun god, who travelled across the sky every day in a *barque* (boat).

Serqet The goddess of scorpions. She was believed to cure the stings and bites of all dangerous creatures like snakes and scorpions.

Seth The brother of Osiris, the god of chaos, evil and the Red Land (the desert). He was shown with the head of a strange dog-like creature that has never been identified.

Sobek The ancient Egyptian crocodile god. On the whole, he was feared by the Egyptians, but he was sometimes seen as a god of fertility, too. There were two big cult temples to Sobek – one in the north, and one south of Waset at a place that is now called Kom Ombo. But there were also sacred crocodile pools and smaller shrines dotted along the Nile, as I've described in the story.

Tawaret A hippopotamus goddess who protected

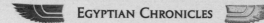
children and women, particularly during childbirth. Like Bes, Tawaret was worshipped in people's homes rather than in temples.

Thoth The god of writing and scribes. He was shown as an ibis, or with the head of an ibis.

GLOSSARY

acacia A small, thorny tree. Some types of acacia grow particularly well in dry, desert regions.

alabaster A whitish stone that is quite soft and easily carved. The Egyptians used it to make many beautiful objects.

amulet A lucky charm, worn to protect a person from evil.

carnelian A reddish stone used by the Egyptians to make jewellery.

clerestory window A window set high in a wall to let in some light. Only big houses had windows – most people's houses were very dark inside to keep them cool.

deben A measurement of what things were worth. There was no money in ancient Egypt – people bought things with grain or just swapped one item for another. But they estimated how much things were worth in *deben*, usually of copper. Gold was much more valuable.

Djeba (You say 'Jay-ba') This is one of the ancient

names for the site of the cult temple of Horus, south of Waset. Today it is called Edfu. (See the section on Egypt's temples.)

doum palm A kind of palm tree that grows along the River Nile. Its fruits are much bigger than dates (which grow on a different kind of palm), and many have been found in ancient Egyptian tombs. (Sometimes written **dom** or **doom palm**.)

emmer wheat The type of wheat that was grown in ancient Egypt. Barley was the other main food crop.

frankincense A kind of tree resin that was used to make incense and perfumes.

hieratic A shorthand version of hieroglyphics, which simplified the hieroglyphs to make them quicker to write.

hieroglyphics The system of ancient Egyptian picture writing. Each individual picture is called a **hieroglyph**.

Imhotep A very famous architect, doctor and engineer who lived in the Old Kingdom, about 1,400 years before the time of Isis and Hopi. He was so clever that later Egyptians worshipped him as a god. No wonder Tutmose thought it was a good name to choose!

lapis lazuli A deep blue semi-precious stone that the Egyptians valued highly. It wasn't found in Egypt, but had to be imported from modern-day Afghanistan.

limestone Along with sandstone, this was a rock commonly found in Egypt and used to build the many temples (but not houses, which were made of mud brick).

lotus Lotus flowers were actually blue water lilies that

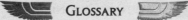

grew along the Nile. Their flowers open in the morning and close at night, so they were seen as a symbol of the rising and setting sun, and the cycle of creation. They were used in perfume, and were believed to have healing powers, too.

ma'at The ancient Egyptian principle of divine justice and order. The principle was represented by a goddess of the same name.

mercenary Someone who hires himself out as a soldier. Unlike most soldiers, who fight for their country or government, mercenaries fight for whoever is paying them.

myrrh A kind of tree sap or resin that has a powerful smell. The ancient Egyptians used it to make incense and to perfume their oils.

Next World The place ancient Egyptians believed they would go after death. It would be better than this world, of course, but quite similar – which was why they needed to take their bodies and many possessions with them.

obelisk A tall, narrow granite spike that was often erected in temples.

ostracon (pl. **ostraca**) A small piece of pottery or a flake of limestone used as 'scrap paper' for writing on.

papyrus A kind of reed that used to grow in the marshes alongside the Nile, especially in the Delta region to the north. It was made into many things – mats, baskets, sandals and even boats – but it is most famous for the flat sheets of 'paper' made from it, which are named after the reed.

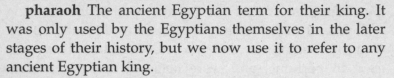

pharaoh The ancient Egyptian term for their king. It was only used by the Egyptians themselves in the later stages of their history, but we now use it to refer to any ancient Egyptian king.

prow The front of a boat.

scarab A kind of dung beetle that was worshipped by the Egyptians. Scarab amulets were thought to give great protection. The scarab was the creature of the god Khepri (see the Gods and Goddesses section).

stern The back of a boat.

temple Temples were a very important focus for the ancient Egyptian religion. There were cult temples for the worship of a particular god, and mortuary temples for the worship of a king after his death. (See the section on Egypt's Temples.)

turquoise A green-blue semi-precious stone that was mined by the Egyptians in Sinai. They used it to make beautiful objects, inlays and jewellery.

Isis and Hopi's story continues
as they prepare for an important festival,
where they will perform for the king in

THE SACRED SCARAB

Read on for an exciting extract . . .

EGYPTIAN CHRONICLES

THE
SACRED
SCARAB

Very carefully, Hopi applied an ointment of mashed onion and salt to the farmer's arm. The man winced as the mash went on, then held his arm stiffly as Hopi wrapped a bandage around it.

'Will I live?' the farmer asked, his voice quaking.

Hopi grinned. 'Oh yes, you'll be fine.' He looked up at Menna. 'Won't he, Menna?'

The old priest of Serqet sighed. 'Yes, yes. This snake is harmless.'

'Harmless? But its teeth sank deep into my arm!' exclaimed the farmer.

'Trust me,' said Menna wearily, 'I see plenty of these bites at harvest time. The snake was hiding in a sheaf of wheat, am I right?'

'Yes, yes, but . . .' The farmer looked dubious. 'You are sure, then?'

'Perfectly sure. Keep the ointment on until tomorrow, then unwrap the bandage. The bite will soon heal.'

The farmer stared at his arm, as though he could scarcely believe his luck. Then he scratched his head with his good arm, and stood up. 'I must pay you,' he said. 'I have brought grain.'

'Grain is always welcome,' said Menna. 'Though the gods know I can't seem to eat very much these days.'

The farmer indicated the bag that he had by his side. 'I hope this is enough.'

'Indeed. May the gods be with you.'

Hopi took in Menna's tired eyes and hunched shoulders as he showed the farmer out of Menna's house. This was the busiest time of the year, but his tutor was not himself. With every new patient who arrived to receive treatment, he seemed a little more weary, a little more depressed. Hopi knew he was grieving the death of his brother, but it seemed to have affected him very deeply.

Menna returned to the courtyard. 'I'm afraid there will be no more treatments today,' he said, wiping his forehead. 'You may go, Hopi. There is something I must do.'

Hopi scrambled to his feet. 'Can't I help you, Menna?'

The old man shook his head. 'I must visit the family tomb. It is over the river on the west bank.'

This was intriguing news. 'I could carry your bag,' Hopi offered.

Menna smiled. 'I can see you won't take no for an answer. Very well, Hopi. Thank you. Fetch me my cloak – I may feel a chill on the river.'

Hopi did as his tutor told him, and they were soon making their way through the winding streets of Waset. Menna had a bad back and walked with a stoop, while Hopi had a limp from the day he had been attacked by crocodiles, so they didn't hurry. Hopi wandered along by his tutor's side, thinking. He knew that Menna's brother was lying in the embalmers' workshops, his body slowly drying out in natron salt. That should have been enough to tell him that Menna's family was rich – most people couldn't afford to give their loved ones such special treatment. But Menna had always seemed humble, and his house was not at all grand, so Hopi hadn't given it much thought. This was different – a family tomb on the west bank was impressive.

They reached the riverbank, where a ferry shunted to and fro across the Nile. Hopi helped Menna on board, and they sat waiting for the boat to fill up.

Menna seemed to be thinking, too. He turned to

Hopi, placing a hand on his knee. 'I am growing old,' he said quietly. 'It is good that you have come with me.'

'You know I'd do anything to help,' said Hopi.

'Yes,' the old man sighed. 'You're a good apprentice. You have already learned much. But there are some lessons that only the gods can teach.'

Hopi looked at him. 'What sort of lessons?'

Menna shook his head. 'You will learn, Hopi, you will learn. I must ensure that you do, before it is too late. For the time being, it is good that you will see my tomb, for I, too, will lie there one day.'

The ferry started to glide across the Nile. Hopi gazed across the water at the west bank, where the barren mountains of the desert rose up against the blue sky. This was the Kingdom of the Dead, where people were taken to meet the Next World. He was burning with curiosity, and a little fear, too. He didn't like to think of Menna's death, or of anything being *too late*.

THE SACRED SCARAB
by Gill Harvey
COMING SOON